Arnost

Shelley Weiner was born in South Africa and is of Lithuanian descent. She has lived in London since 1977 with her husband and two children. An experienced journalist and teacher of creative writing, she has written three acclaimed novels: *A Sister's Tale*, *The Last Honeymoon* and *The Joker.*

The cover of this book incorporates *Head of a Man* by T[illegible]loff.

ARNOST

a reconciliation

SHELLEY WEINER

STARHAVEN

in association with

ejps

THE EUROPEAN JEWISH PUBLICATION SOCIETY

For my father

First published in 2001 by Starhaven
in association with The European Jewish Publication Society,
PO Box 19948, London N3 3ZJ. Website: www.ejps.org.uk

ISBN 0-936315-18-0

STARHAVEN, 42 Frognal, London NW3 6AG
in U.S., c/o Box 2573, La Jolla, CA 92038, USA
email: starhaven@aesthesia.co.uk

Typeset in Weidemann by John Mallinson
Printed by CPI Copyspeed, 38 Ballard's Lane, London N3 2BJ

The European Jewish Publication Society is a registered charity which gives grants to assist in the publication and distribution of books relevant to Jewish literature, history, religion, philosophy, politics and culture.

I.

Helena rises to speak. 'Friends,' she begins. The hubbub subsides as eyes turn towards her.

All except four.

It is a charity dinner in the ballroom of a top London hotel and the gathering is rich and influential and visibly enchanted by Helena's sincerity, dignity and charm. 'It is most good-hearted, most generous of you to have braved this cold weather to be here,' she says, aware that the accumulation of chequebooks and credit cards has far less to do with benevolence than with her persuasive powers. As the current Honorary Chair of seven fund-raising committees, she has the influence and tenacity to muster a guest list envied by charity organisers throughout the land. Now, having released a rush of well-being and united her audience in magnanimity and mutual stoicism, she introduces the sympathetic celebrity – a mandatory presence on an occasion such as this. He is a media historian with right-wing leanings who hasn't realised until this evening how passionately he feels about his obscure ethnic roots.

Which is fortunate indeed for tonight's pressing cause: the establishment of a Jewish Heritage Museum in an old synagogue in London's East End. With a flourish the celebrity launches the fund – 'Tradition 2000' – amidst enthusiastic applause.

There are two members of the audience, however, whose hands are quite still. They are staring at one another, eyes captured in a mutual gaze as though each has seen a ghost.

'Friends,' concludes Helena, gliding effortlessly to the votes of thanks. 'Dear friends...'

The eyes disengage. One of the pair – conspicuously older and more shabbily attired – starts murmuring to a woman at his side. The other forces his attention back to the platform in time to hear Helena's deep appreciation for the support of her dear long-suffering husband, Arnold.

Arnold?

He starts.

Who is Arnold?

This spectral encounter has shaken his identity. He has become another person in another world. With effort, he returns to the present and manages to curve his mouth into an appropriately spousal smile.

2.

As he nods his head, acknowledging Helena's effusive thanks, Arnold is inwardly fuming about his weakness in succumbing to this gathering. Is this what comes out of loyalty to one's wife? Until recently, wild horses wouldn't have dragged him to one of her charity events, and there was always the pressure of business commitments to use as an excuse. Tonight, though, there seemed no way out of it, no argument with her insistence that she needed him at her side and that he would enjoy rubbing shoulders with the rich and powerful. The rich and powerful indeed. If he'd known who was to be included in this supposedly top-notch crowd, nothing would have persuaded him to come.

There he was, feeling self-righteous about his husbandly presence and generally superior to most of his fellow guests. Culturally speaking, of course. He was offering cursory nods to former business competitors and twitches of the mouth to competitors' wives, when suddenly he noticed in the far corner that solitary and shabbily dressed old man whose presence chafed at his sense of order. He resented the uniform prosperity of the assembly being disturbed. Irritated, he looked again at the interloper and stopped short. Unsuccessfully he tried to return his attention to the platform, to Helena's eloquent prattling, telling himself that this was crazy, there were countless people who seemed familiar, doppelgängers…

Then the old man sighed.

And Arnold knew he wasn't mad, for the sigh was unmistakable. There was a particular inclination of the neck, a specific raising of the shoulders, a distinctive exhalation of breath accompanied by a slow shaking of the head. Arnold knew that sigh. He would know it anywhere.

The speeches seem to go on forever. Arnold seeks distraction in his multilingual mental lexicon and tries to find relief in a word.

Attenuated. At-ten-u-ated...

What a wonderfully descriptive term for the drawn-out proceedings, the tedious sequence of thanks and counter-thanks, the pomposity, the empty praise. Arnold has always found solace in word games. During his teens, when he set out to master English, he kept a dictionary in his pocket and consulted it conscientiously when in the slightest doubt. He stored his findings in the expanding vocabulary in his head until he'd built up an inner thesaurus that rendered his pocket book redundant. By then, naming things had become his habit, his portable test of mental acuity, a diversionary tactic that worked when all else failed.

Except now – now that he's recognised the grey-haired old fellow across the room. He tries to find a name for that too – the circuitry of fate, the apparently random crossing and re-crossing of paths. Happenstance? Fluke? What are the odds against bumping up against someone from a former life in a distant country?

The odds? Arnold tightens his mouth, for he knows that he has encountered something more important than a little wager – so disturbingly important that he must employ all his considerable will power to focus on the applause in the wake of his wife's extravagant prose. He searches for another word to express the length and tedium of the evening.

Protracted, he thinks weakly.

How he longs for it to end so that he can escape from the old man's gaze. It is scorching him. His skin prickles. Arnold squirms inwardly but maintains his sardonically aloof demeanour. Not for an instant does he allow it to slip.

Hypocritical, he tries, as he attempts to match his smile with the general expressions of self-satisfaction surrounding him. 'Excuse me, please.' With curt politeness he makes his way towards the platform, towards Helena at the centre of a congratulatory huddle. People greet him and stand aside. They reserve their warmth for Helena and their respect for Arnold, which is the way he wants it. Respect – esteem –

deference, he thinks as he reaches his wife. His itch has abated and he no longer squirms.

'You spoke extremely well my dear,' he says in his slow, measured voice.

'Did I?' She's flushed and exhilarated, revelling in the attention. Arnold expects her euphoria to last well into the night. She'll chatter compulsively, reliving her success, and at some point will marvel at how lucky she is. *Terribly* lucky, is the way she will put it. Arnold has noticed how widely that phrase is used. He doesn't believe in luck. Some people have certain advantages over others, naturally, but luck is mostly something one makes. Arnold certainly hasn't achieved what he has by relying on luck.

'Do you think we'll be able to leave quite soon?' he asks. He is about to say something about the busy schedule awaiting him tomorrow but is aware that apart from his weekly duplicate bridge session there are now few demands on his time. 'I'm rather tired,' he complains instead. He has an urgent desire to be away from this babbling mob – to be at home, asleep.

'Poor Arnold,' she soothes. 'This must be so tedious for you.'

'No,' he objects quickly. 'Not at all.'

'We'll be off in a minute. I'd just like to have a quick word with Betty Wilson about arranging an Exec meeting. Now the vital question is: have I brought my diary along with me?'

He hovers, barely hiding his impatience, struggling to resist the impulse to extend his gaze to the far end of the room. He could have been wrong. In fact, it was highly likely that he was wrong. He'll steal a glance surreptitiously.

'Isn't this exciting?' someone exclaims. 'The possibilities this museum opens up – goodness! Now we need a computer expert – a website person, CD-ROM, that sort of thing.'

Arnold, squinting, can't locate him. The stranger. The oddity who might or might not be. It seems he has left, whoever he was. A figment of his imagination, in all likelihood. A *chimera*, he thinks, exhaling in relief. A *mirage*...

Someone meanwhile is nudging past him towards the cluster round Helena. Arnold mutters crossly, for he hates being jostled. 'I'm sorry,' says the offender without taking his eyes off his destination. Idiot, thinks Arnold, watching him head for his wife, hearing his greeting and the effusive response. 'Bernard! How nice to see you. Everyone, this is Bernard Kaplan, the new Cantor. Bernard's going to do wonderful things for the museum – in addition to leading synagogue services, of course. He has all sorts of ideas.'

'Actually,' says Bernard – and Arnold notices how close he stands to Helena, how intently he is regarding her. The man is obnoxious. 'Actually, I overheard someone saying you were looking for a person who was keen on computers and... well, if I could be of any assistance?'

An enthusiastic chorus greets his words and Arnold can't refrain from an impatient clearing of his throat. 'Helena, dear,' he prompts. Hasn't he told her he is tired? 'Helena,' he repeats in case she hasn't heard. Surely she wouldn't be so attentive to this absurd Bernard if she were aware that her husband was addressing her? He edges forward and places a hand on her shoulder. She starts and turns towards him, frowning. 'In a minute, Arnold,' she says as though reprimanding a child.

Or that's the way it seems to Arnold, who recoils in anger and embarrassment. How could she? How dare she? A woman her age blatantly flirting with a stranger, showing such disrespect to her husband. Insupportable, he thinks. Unacceptable. Totally inappropriate. He seethes but stays silent, a determined half-smile hurting his face. His body is taut.

Hours pass, it seems, before she finally takes leave of her acolytes and allows Arnold to assist her with her coat, and eventually they step into the street.

At last they reach home. Arnold, entering the immaculately maintained Chelsea residence (four beds, three receps, fine position off Onslow Square), is able to breathe normally again. *Deliverance*, he thinks, surveying his domain and inhaling its sense of permanence and grandeur. A house which announces – discreetly, of course – that its master is a man of substance, a man to be reckoned with.

Not that Arnold generally has to go about proving his stature. This evening, however, has churned him up. He reminds himself that this was his first public appearance as a man of leisure and thus understandable for him to feel strange. Retirement is a new situation and calls for adjustment. Which he'll manage, of course, for adaptability has always been one of his strengths. Didn't people marvel time after time – aren't they marvelling still? – about the rapidity and ease with which he became an Englishman? 'How did you manage it, Arnold?' they'd ask. 'Some people remain foreigners, outsiders, all their lives.' Simple, he would answer, quoting the motto, the little aphorism, that he has always applied to business and pleasure – to life: Look ahead. He succeeded by looking ahead and intends to keep looking ahead.

Except that suddenly the view seems to have gone hazy.

But that's temporary, he tells himself. A passing mist. Soon it will rise and the scenery of his future will be revealed. After all, the scenery of the present – his affluence, his social standing – was once a distant ambition. And now, look at what he has achieved.

'You're rather quiet tonight,' Helena observes. She has exchanged her designer suit for the floral kimono she wears indoors. Arnold, suddenly attentive, sees that she looks old and unglamorous without her trappings. For some reason this pleases him.

'Just introspective,' he says vaguely. 'And, as I said, tired.'

'How about some cocoa?' She jumps up, heading for the kitchen without awaiting his response. 'That's what you need. A nice, hot, comforting cup of cocoa. I think I'll join you – I've hardly had a thing all day, so I can afford the extra calories.'

Cups clatter. She hums – a high tuneless sound that makes Arnold wince. Cocoa, he thinks with sudden nausea – the beverage of the old, the sick, the dependent. So that's what he faces: Helena being fêted and then consoling him with cocoa. Sharply he calls her name.

'What is it?' She emerges from the kitchen.

'Actually, dear,' he says, 'I think I'll pass on the cocoa.' He pauses, rubbing his forehead. 'But you go ahead – please do. I'll pour myself a small whisky to keep you company.'

She returns to the kitchen, no longer humming.

Her ebullience, however, isn't dampened for long. Arnold wonders what it would take to extinguish his wife's indomitable *joie de vivre* and then wonders why he should be wondering such a thing. And while he is wondering and counter-wondering she is chattering away – reliving every moment of her glorious evening.

'I *must* ring Betty to find out where the donations stand… What's the time?' She glances at her watch. 'Ten thirty. Far too late – for *Betty*. Goodness, Arnold, isn't she looking dreadful? She has really let herself go. Did you notice her funny little husband, Norman? It's hilarious the way she talks about him as though he's a matinee idol. Oh, do you think it's too late to give Sandra a call? She was slightly worried about William this morning – thought he might be sickening for something…'

She ponders and he shrugs, for her questions at a time like this are strictly rhetorical. The whisky meanwhile is doing its work. The knot in his belly is unravelling.

'No,' she continues decisively, 'I'll talk to her tomorrow. I'm sure it can't be anything serious – she'd have let us know. Isn't William gorgeous, though? I'd never say it to the others – even to Sandra. He really is the pick of our little lot, don't you think?'

He nods, swallowing deeply, pleasantly aware of the warmth slipping down his throat and filling his body.

'I suppose I shouldn't say that – it isn't fair. They're *all* lovely – every one of them. In fact…'

Wait for it, thinks Arnold. The inevitable paean to her good fortune:

'…as I keep reminding myself, we've been blessed with them. Truly. I know Evie has her ups and downs, but on the whole – honestly, when one thinks about the suffering in this world, we've been so *terribly* lucky.'

She sucks contemplatively on a finger that she's dipped into her cocoa, an inelegance she would never permit herself in other company. Arnold studies her with alcohol-assisted tolerance and waits for the coda.

'When I compare our situation with that poor old man, for

instance…'

Not that, thinks Arnold. Smug pity is sweeping her to dangerous ground. He wants to distract her, to deflect her flow. Instead he hears himself asking: 'Which old man?'

Immediately he regrets the question. Despite the whisky, he feels a prickle of unease. What made him open his mouth? He drains his glass hastily and is about to insist that they go to bed. Immediately. He has been exhausted for hours and badly needs to get to sleep. If he isn't careful, his psoriasis will flare.

But Helena won't be deterred. 'Didn't you spot him?'

'Who?'

'The elderly man in that threadbare jacket? Honestly, Arnold, you're not quite with us this evening. And I don't think you ought to be drinking whisky – it isn't good for you.'

He makes a dismissive gesture that converts itself into a yawn, but before he can escape she has returned to the plight of 'that poor old man'. 'Surely you noticed him?' she insists. 'Everyone did. There was hardly a person in the room who didn't want to know who he was and where he came from, et cetera.'

'And?' asks Arnold, unable to restrain himself despite the apprehension that is regaining its hold on his innards.

'I'm not quite sure – I tried to find out. No one seems to know where he was *originally* from, but he's been the synagogue caretaker for God-knows-how-many years.'

'I see,' says Arnold, who doesn't. Surely there are worse fates than that of long-term caretaker? Who gives a damn anyway? All he wants is to be in bed, asleep. What on earth made him open his mouth? Hasn't he learnt by now that Helena is unstoppable once she gets going?

'The thing is,' she continues, clearly blind to her husband's restlessness and his need to retire, 'nobody seems to be quite sure what to do about him now that the museum project is going ahead. They need his flat as a residence for the curator, and I believe they've offered him a place in a home. He's none too keen on that. Lily Sanderson insisted that he should be asked to the reception as a gesture of goodwill – the poor man. Honestly, he looked too pathetic for words.'

Arnold makes for the doorway, slowly inching forward. His head is reeling and he is barely managing to keep his composure. 'Good night,' he says in a clipped voice.

'Oh – nighty-night, Arnold. I'll be up in a minute. What a day it's been – people have no idea what a strain it is to be the centre of attention. One can't afford to lapse for a second... Oh, did you notice that sweet young man? Bernard. The new Cantor. So obliging – and quite nice looking too, don't you think?'

He reaches the summit of the stairs, desperate to escape her voice. But it pursues him, its lightness belying a tenacity which he fails to outpace.

'I think we should ask him over some time. Apparently his wife's a real battle-axe – terribly orthodox – wouldn't eat a thing here, so we can't ask them for a meal. I'm sure he wouldn't mind coming on his own, though – for coffee, if nothing else.'

He wants to jam two fingers into his ears and hum loudly, the way Evie once did when he tried to lecture her on her errant ways. He almost hit her then – the first time ever, the only time. He shook with rage and very nearly lost control. But he managed to take a grip on himself, for Arnold Rose was always in control.

His tablets. He needs his sleeping pills and perhaps an antihistamine in case the itch returns. He cannot risk insomnia tonight. 'Helena,' he calls, for her monologue has abated. His voice, miraculously, sounds steady, normal. 'Helena, when you come upstairs, would you please bring up a glass of water? I seem to have forgotten.'

There is silence. Arnold suddenly realises how unusual his request is, how very unlike him it is to have forgotten. He is usually meticulous about everyday things and scathing about the lapses of others. Ah well. Even he can make an occasional mistake. It's due to circumstances, he tells himself – circumstances beyond his control.

'Are you sure you're all right?' Helena appears at the door, glass in hand.

'Fine thank you.' Stiffly, he accepts it.

She studies him. 'You don't look right. I wish you hadn't had all that whisky – it's not good for you.'

'I'm perfectly well – I need to get to bed, that's all.' Irritably he extracts his tablets from their containers and places them on his bedside table alongside his glass. Then he draws out his pyjamas, neatly folded, from beneath his pillow and embarks on his nightly retirement routine. By the time he has flossed his teeth and urinated he feels better. The medication will make him feel better still. He will lie back, gaze at a newspaper or an article in *The Economist* perhaps, and watch the words blurring, their coherence floating out of reach, as in a dream.

Tonight, though, the drugs are ineffective. Arnold stares at the words which remain razor-sharp before his eyes and tries to swallow the apprehension rising like bile in his throat. His neck itches. His head hurts. Soon Helena will return upstairs and if he isn't asleep she will fuss and chatter, fuss and chatter. He tries to remember the exact dosage he has taken – was it ten milligrams of temazepam or twenty? And the antihistamine? Which antihistamine? How can he have forgotten? Don't panic, he tells himself, putting aside the magazine and tightly shutting his eyes. He will empty his mind – forcibly expel that inexplicable anxiety which is unsteadying him so and hampering the action of his medication.

But he can't. Hard as he tries, he is unable to banish the images that have taken occupation of his head. A sigh. An old man's sigh. An old-young sigh – weary, accusing, all-knowing.

And something else: a frown. A vexed impatient frown and a bitingly angry voice. '*In a minute, Arnold.*' Who said that? Helena? No, no – long before, in another life, a part of his life that he once lopped off. Now like the severed limb of an amputee, it has begun to itch unbearably. He reaches for another tablet. Surely there must be a remedy strong enough to ease this awful itch?

He lies back and, with a sigh of relief, feels the onset of the only infallible distraction from his chronic psoriasis. His itch abates as his mind is flooded with a rush of remembered light.

3.

It's the light of his Eden, the light that once glowed from the sky and from his mother's face, dappling and dancing beneath the apple trees, until darkness fell and the world grew bleak and cold with the icy abruptness of her voice.

'In a minute...'

She didn't say Arnold, though, for he wasn't Arnold then. She called him Arnost.

'In a minute, Arnost,' she snapped.

Arnost.

He shudders, struggling to hold on to the safe oblivion of the present, but unable to withstand the force of the recollection. 'Mother, please...' He feels his lips shaping the invocation, even as he tells himself that after all this time it doesn't matter – the chiaroscuro of memory is illusion. Surely there was shadow in the time he remembers as uninterrupted light? And surely the sun shone again afterwards? Anyway, she is long gone. Dead. Nothing left of her at all. 'Oh, Mother...'

There was Julis before the darkness. Julis the chick who became Julis the hen.

'She's your very own,' said Mother, presenting him with a ball of soft sunflower fluff, a downy handful that outgrew his pocket and outlived his father. When Father died, they lit candles and turned the mirrors to the wall while plump-laying Julis continued to strut in the yard. Arnost took refuge with his hen.

It wasn't then that the darkness came. Not for the loss of poor Father, who had been sick forever, it seemed. Shivering, sweating, calling for broth and water and poultices and cloths. The War, they said. He had caught malaria while defending Hungary on the ghastly Russian front. How hard for Rosa to have to nurse him and take care of the shop. And, of course, the child. The boy. Not that she complained about him, for her Arnost was no trouble. On the contrary, she often declared (Arnost's heart swelled when he heard it) what a help he was. He was her companion, her little man. What would she have done without small Arnost? How would she have managed if he hadn't been there to answer her bidding and amuse the customers and make her laugh and bring her tea?

She held him tight when Father died. She held Arnost and Arnost held Julis, and although he felt obliged to look sad, the sun continued to shine. It didn't seem to matter that the shelves in the shop and the shelves in the kitchen and even the apple trees were bare. Or that the chickens – apart from Julis – were scrawny and the coal-store empty and the autumn nights chill. None of that mattered. Not to Arnost.

Mother cried though. She cried ceaselessly, shedding endless tears that rinsed the lustre from her eyes and made them soggy – great heaving sobs during which she implored God, the angels, even the spirit of dead Father for help. What would become of them? What could she do?

'Don't worry,' he assured her with the certainty of innocence, for what did poverty or hunger matter in the golden light of his paradise? 'It will be all right, Mother. Everything will be all right.'

And it was. Before very long her saviour Tamás appeared. Large, healthy Tamás, who stocked the shelves and revived the chickens. He made the apple trees burgeon with luscious fruit and Arnost's mother swell with new life. At first, the Elysian brightness remained undimmed. In a strange and ominous way it glowed brighter than ever, while Arnost clung to the belief that he was more important to his mother than the crass and robust newcomer.

But then, like a hammer-blow, came her dismissive 'in a minute' – and darkness descended.

'Mother – please, *please...*'

'What is it? Can't you see that I'm busy? There's the laundry to be done and Tamás's dinner and my feet, my poor feet...'

'It's Julis – she's gone.'

'Gone?'

'She isn't there – in the yard – where she usually is.'

'Oh. Oh, well...'

'Mother, did you hear what I said? Julis has gone – she's disappeared.'

'Honestly, Arnost – such a fuss about a chicken. You're a big boy now. Come inside – it's getting dark.'

Later he discovered that Julis had stopped laying and Tamás had decided to kill her. Tamás had killed her and Mother had cooked her. Julis's liver had been chopped, her flesh had been boiled and her carcass used to make broth.

Arnost steadfastly refused to eat.

'You're being silly,' Tamás jeered. 'Isn't he, Rosa? You've spoilt him – I always said you did. A hen that won't lay is only fit for the pot – no point in being sentimental.'

Arnost didn't respond. He watched his mother and Tamás exchanging meaningful glances and grew cold inside. It was as though a source of radiant heat had been extinguished and all that remained was a hard black core.

'Stop sulking,' said Mother. 'You can have another chick.'

'I don't want one.' His voice was level and composed. 'I'm too old for that now.'

He was ten. He remembers the consciousness of being ten and crossing from light into darkness. The anger, the fear, the determination to find his way, to outstare the gloom until a path could be discerned. Who cared about a stupid hen? Tamás was right – there wasn't any point in being sentimental. As for her, his mother... Arnost managed to hold back tears, making sure that no one saw his silent struggle. As for Mother – he regretted losing her allegiance, but there was nothing to be done about it. Unless, of course, he found himself another mother.

He smiled at the idea – a new, cynical smile that seemed to defy the dusk but somehow made people uncomfortable. He noticed the way his classmates would back off when he approached, the wariness of his teachers. Nobody remarked on it, though, for he remained impeccably polite – and quite glad of the space they cleared around him. It made his exit route easier to discern.

The way out. From boring little Nyirbátor with its chickens and apple trees and small town preoccupations; from Mother and Tamás and their twins and whatever other progeny grew in her reinflated belly. From the dark and the cold.

'Arnold – you're shivering.'

He blinks in confusion and for a moment fails to recognise her – Helena, bending over him, fragrantly replete with her cosmetic armour. Anti-Sagging Cream frosts her face and Arnold, jolted into the present, turns away.

'What is the matter?' she wants to know.

'I was asleep,' he lies.

'You were shivering,' she insists. 'I saw you.'

'It's cold.'

'It is, isn't it? *Really* cold for this time of year. But it's unlike you to feel it so badly, Arnold. You always boast that you're immune to the cold. Don't you think that perhaps you ought to get yourself checked out?'

He mumbles something vague, wishing she would go away.

'In fact,' she continues, 'you should go and see Malcolm. Shall I make an appointment for you? It will be much easier now that you're free during the day.'

Free, he thinks. Free, unfettered, unrestrained – liberated from the chains of employment to enjoy unbounded communion with his GP. Is this what he has worked for? Is this what he has come to? 'Good night, Helena,' he says impatiently. He hates her fussing but, in truth, he does feel strange. Maybe it isn't such a bad idea to have a check-up. It won't harm, at any rate. Perhaps there's something new on the market for his skin. Not that Malcolm the genius will be likely to have heard about it. In fact the sensible thing would be for Arnold to find another doctor, some-one he can trust and respect. Someone he can count on.

'Night,' she is saying, assuming her position for repose. It has been choreographed for minimum damage to her coiffure.

Arnold sighs and turned over. At least he can rely upon Helena, whose dedication to good works, good looks and a good marriage hasn't flagged over more than forty years. Unsurprisingly, for steadfastness was the quality that attracted him to her from the start. He knew exactly what he was doing when he proposed to her. Amazing, wasn't it, that even as a newcomer he had picked her out so instinctively, so unerringly? He'd always had a nose for the sort of character who wouldn't let him down. If only he'd been able to choose his mother...

He pulls the blankets closely round him, for he suddenly feels cold again. Those damn tablets. Why aren't they working? Why is oblivion eluding him? He shouldn't still be engaging in this useless, most untypical introspection. Choose his mother, indeed.

His mouth curves disdainfully in the dark and he waits for relief to come with his sneer. The inner hardening that will transform the shivering into cool resolve. Choose his mother...

But he *did* choose his mother. The minute he set eyes on his landlady, Yetta Fine, he decided that she would do.

'Poor boy,' said Yetta, greeting him at the door. 'You're soaked – come inside, out of the rain. Put on some dry clothes and I'll give you something warm to drink.'

'Thank you.'

Even then he knew his manners. Particularly then. He was twelve, underdeveloped with a treble voice, a slip of a boy with the determination of a full-grown man. He had toughened himself against the indifference of his mother, her alliance with Tamás and her absorption in the new babies. He had convinced himself that it didn't matter, she didn't matter, he didn't really need a family after all. Single-mindedly he had set about his escape from Nyirbátor and worked unstintingly until he had secured a place at the academic high school in Nyíregháza, the nearest large town.

Nyíregháza, only thirty-five kilometres from the village of his birth, was worlds away. It was the capital of the region and, compared with Nyirbátor, a metropolis. Yetta's modest house, where Arnost had been billeted as a paying guest, seemed like a palace to a boy who had only known the squalid quarters behind a struggling village shop.

'I am very glad to be here – most honoured,' he said with deep fervour, smiling endearingly. He had made up his mind that Yetta would find him irresistibly sweet.

And she did. It was clear from the start that Yetta was taken with her charming young boarder. She showed him his room and watched with evident gratification the wonder on his face. My room, he thought. A whole room to myself. 'It's beautiful. Thank you.' He stood at the doorway while she bustled in to plump the pillows and straighten the mat.

'There. All ready for you. Settle down – unpack your bag – make yourself warm and dry while I prepare the supper.'

He nodded, overcome by the warmth of his welcome and the grandeur of his accommodation. 'Thank you,' he repeated.

Gently she took his hand. 'You don't have to thank me all the time. I need the rent, you have a place to stay, a good arrangement.'

He agreed. An excellent arrangement. He sat on the bed to contemplate the room and noticed a row of Hebrew books on a corner shelf. Briefly he wondered who had previously lived here. Very briefly, though, for he was set on making it his own.

By the time Yetta called to say supper was ready, he had changed, unpacked and meticulously organised his few possessions. The Hebrew volumes, being battered and untidy, were firmly pushed aside.

Four places were set at the kitchen table.

'Ah – here you are,' said Yetta, when he appeared at the door. 'Rachel – this is Arnost.'

He saw a girl his age, or perhaps a year or two younger. A pale dark-haired girl who was regarding him with interest. Arnost suddenly felt ill at ease: a strange child in a strange house in a strange town in the company of someone who clearly belonged. He cleared his throat uncomfortably.

'Come and sit down,' Yetta urged, and he gratefully complied. He averted his gaze from Rachel, who seemed bent on serving supper, and concentrated instead on the tantalising cooking smells, and the comforting sight of Yetta.

'I hope you eat chicken,' she was saying. 'Most people do. I thought it would be a safe choice.'

Chicken. He hesitated for a moment, hardly more than that, and during that moment everything flashed before him: his mother, Tamás, Julis. He hadn't touched chicken since then. Not a morsel of poultry had passed his lips. But now things had changed; it was a new time and a new place. 'I love chicken,' he said firmly. 'It's my favourite food.'

With as much enthusiasm as he could muster, he drew the first forkful to his mouth. 'It's good,' he forced himself to say, for Yetta was watching him anxiously.

'I'm glad. You look like you can do with some nourishing food. We'll feed him up, won't we Rachel?'

Rachel nodded, silently slipping into her seat. The fourth place was still unoccupied and Arnost was about to ask about it when the front door opened noisily and an icy draught gusted through the house.

'Hershel,' said Yetta in an exasperated voice. 'Hershel, where have you been? We had to start supper without you.'

A tall thin boy made his entrance. Arnost studied him curiously. He clearly wasn't old, this Hershel. Probably thirteen or fourteen – not much older than Arnost himself. Yet there was something about his demeanour that signified great maturity. The weariness of his stance, perhaps, or the way his shabby clothing hung on his frame, or the mournfulness of the blue eyes that peered at Arnost from behind wire spectacles.

'It's ridiculous how you lose your sense of time,' Yetta muttered, handing him his food. 'I particularly asked you to come home early and help me with the room.'

'I'm sorry.' He accepted the plate and, with his head bowed, softly recited a prayer. Then, sitting down, he expelled an enormous sigh.

And Arnost watched, intrigued, for never before had he witnessed such a heartfelt sigh. He noticed the inclination of Hershel's neck, the way he raised his shoulders and slowly shook his head from side to side as he exhaled…

That sigh, that sigh. Surely a simple if distinctive release of breath should have disappeared down the years? Hurricanes dwindle to breezes. They dissipate and leave no trace. Great thunderstorms rage and then die.

How is it possible that a displacement of air so small can have endured over decades and a continent, to taunt him across a crowded room and even follow him to bed?

Arnold listens to Helena's even breathing beside him, and tries to match his respiration to hers. In, out, in, out. Relax, he tells himself. No more voices or rogue gestures. No more wallowing in the past. Look ahead. Breathe steadily and smoothly and keep looking resolutely ahead.

4.

The next morning early, Helena is on the telephone to Betty Wilson. 'No, truly,' she protests when Betty praises the aplomb with which she conducted last night's do. 'It may have *seemed* as though I was in control, but really I can't tell you how nervous I was...' She pauses to hear Betty's reiteration of her tribute. 'I *must* go,' she says at last. 'I'd love to share a good long gossip but – honestly – the things that accumulate when one devotes oneself to a single project! It'll take me *weeks* to catch up.'

Having thus disposed of Betty ('If only that woman's enthusiasm were matched by her intelligence,' she remarks bitchily as she puts down the phone), Helena turns to Arnold who – with great gusto, considering his agitation of the night before – is attending to his breakfast. 'I'd avoid so much butter if I were you,' she says, observing with disapproval the lavish amounts he is applying to his toast.

'Why?' he demands, daring her to suggest that his heart or his weight are at risk. If not for his skin problem (which is by its very nature superficial), Arnold regards himself as an exemplary specimen – even compared with someone half his age. 'Since when do *I* have to watch what I eat?'

She doesn't rise to the challenge. She merely shrugs and pours tea. 'It's so sad,' she says out of the blue.

'What's sad?' he asks, feeling a prickle of apprehension and wishing she would leave him to his breakfast. If she insists on playing Lady Bountiful, that's fine. He, on the other hand, merely wants to live quietly and unobtrusively, without harming anyone.

'Imagine it,' says Helena, adding lemon to her tea and frowning compassionately. She perfected this facial expression several years ago during a stretch of voluntary work for a hospice.

'What *are* you going on about?' Arnold's irritation has superseded his unease for he has always found Helena in philanthropic mode unbearable. He much prefers her bossy.

'The old man – that caretaker we were talking about last night, remember?'

Arnold remembers all too well and tries to change the subject. 'How is William today?' he asks.

'Fine – much better – Sandra says it was a false alarm,' she replies distractedly, maintaining her expression of gloomy sympathy. Arnold wants to point out the irreversible damage she might be doing to her complexion but thinks it best to stay silent. 'The girls,' she adds, shaking her head, 'are terribly upset.'

'About William?'

'Arnold, don't be ridiculous. About the caretaker. Betty says her phone hasn't stopped ringing. Apparently *everyone* noticed him at the reception – I could *kill* that Lily Sanderson for inviting him.'

Me too, thinks Arnold. He means it.

'Not that I don't feel sorry for him,' she continues. 'I do – desperately. But the whole business is not going to do the project any good, *that's* clear.' She tops up her tea. 'The question is whether or not to take steps to persuade the trustees, force them if necessary, to allow the caretaker to stay. It's such bad publicity for us to be seen to be dispossessing a helpless old man. And they say he's *suffered* so...'

Arnold rises to his feet. 'Will you excuse me?' Enough is enough. Being a gentleman of leisure shouldn't mean involvement in his *wife's* leisure pursuits. On the contrary, Arnold has always attributed the success of his marriage to the fact that he and Helena have consistently maintained separate interests. He intends to keep it this way. 'I have things to attend to.'

'Oh?' She sounds surprised. 'But what do you *think*, Arnold?'

'About what?'

'Haven't you been listening? About the *caretaker.* Do you know something? I don't even know the poor soul's name.'

And may it remain that way, thinks Arnold as he leaves the room. May Hershel Fine remain anonymous – and silent. He feels panic rising as he dares to acknowledge the name, even in his head. Quickly he suppresses the panic with anger. Surely the women can find another target for their silly hysterical compassion? Aren't there a million other causes – worthier and less dangerous? Can't they fixate on another old man who is about to be made homeless – anyone, anywhere, other than Hershel Fine?

5.

Hershel meanwhile is similarly disturbed. Not about the swell of female solicitude (of which he is still unaware) but about why he of all people has been singled out for persecution – again. It never ends, he thinks – then smiles ruefully. What else can he do? Sit and cry? Does it matter in the end about the state or location of a person's earthly habitation when not far ahead of him lies the glorious World to Come?

On the other hand, why *shouldn't* he be allowed to remain here during the interim? A palace it's not, with its patches of damp and worn furniture and a toilet you have to talk to nicely before it flushes. Not by any stretch of the imagination can this be called luxurious, but after almost forty years it is home. On the *other* hand…

Hershel shakes his head wearily, for in truth he doesn't care about his living quarters. Not really. Something else has supplanted the accommodation problem as the uppermost thing in his mind. Who would have dreamt…? It *was* a dream. Never mind a dream, a nightmare.

'Who is he?' he asked the busybody, that Lily-what's-her-name, who was nagging him, on and on, about the unlawfulness of his dispossession, his claims on the property. Claims? The only property he had ever claimed was a bag of earth from the Holy Land. Abe Silverstein had brought it back for him from one of his trips for Hershel to bury at his side, thus giving him an easier resurrection, come the Messiah. 'Who is that man?' he whispered, just to make sure.

As though he didn't know. As though he hadn't smelt him from the very minute he walked into the room. A room? Now *that* was a palace. What Hershel Fine was doing there, God only knows. Perhaps He knows only too well. Maybe Divine Providence led him there. Maybe God was a little tired of His routine duties and decided to amuse Himself by organising the whole thing.

Hershel scratches his head, wondering at the heavenly motive for arranging such an encounter. Revenge? Unlikely. Forgiveness, then? Is Hershel being called on to forgive? 'Look here,' he says aloud, palms uplifted in protest. 'This is a bit much to ask of me, it really is...'

It's all very well believing that earthly misery will be rewarded by heavenly bliss, that those who are virtuous and have little can look forward to eternal wealth. Or even that the wicked who prosper are being rewarded for their few good deeds while the saintly who suffer are being punished for their inadvertent sins. All that is fine and good and (God help him) who is Hershel to argue? Not with the theories, anyway. Most of his life he has reflected on theories – giving perfect moral solutions to abstract dilemmas, Talmudic answers to imaginary problems. But this is real. A flesh-and-blood visitation from the past.

'That's Arnold Rose,' said the busybody, following his gaze across the room.

Naturally. Unmistakably. And isn't it typical that he changed his name? As though Arnost Rosenbaum isn't good enough or smart enough or English enough.

'Do you know him?' she whispered.

He shrugged, for it was none of her business.

'That's his wife – over there.' She indicated the platform.

'Ah,' he said meaningfully. 'A*ha*.'

'Do you know her?' she asked eagerly.

'I know the type.'

And now? What is he to do with this knowledge? He has seen how affluent and influential Arnold has become. Healthy as an ox as well. Is Hershel now meant to carry on in his quiet and undemanding way and continue to be grateful for the scraps they give him? Is this a test – yet another test?

And if he passes, what then? His final years in the splendour of – how did they put it? – a 'reputable establishment for Jewish senior citizens'? Hershel shudders at the idea and grows angry. Extremely angry. Angry like he can't remember ever having been before. Breathing hard, and shuffling noisily through some papers stacked under the candlestick on his table, he extracts a letter which he re-reads with a frown:

Dear Mr Fine,

This is to inform you that an extraordinary meeting of the Synagogue Management Board was held last week to make final arrangements for the establishment of a Museum of Jewish Life adjacent to our premises. The project has been placed in the hands of a newly created Board of Trustees and we believe you will be as excited as we are about the possibilities it presents.

Apart from its importance to the preservation of our cultural heritage, the museum will go some way towards easing the synagogue's financial situation which, I have to tell you, has become critical. The Trustees have offered to donate to us a generous lump sum as well as a sizeable contribution towards our monthly overheads. In exchange we have given them assurance of our support for the project. We have also agreed to provide accommodation for a curator of their choice.

This is where, unfortunately, you will be affected, Mr Fine. The accommodation they have in mind is the flat currently being occupied by the synagogue caretaker, i.e. yourself. The Trustees are aware of the situation and have assured us that a) the person they have in mind for the job of curator will be fully qualified to act as caretaker as well; and b) they will make all arrangements for you to live in retirement in a reputable establishment for Jewish senior citizens.

Mr Fine, this is not an easy letter to write. I have been instructed by the Board to emphasise how much your work and presence here have been appreciated over the years. You will be sadly missed and we hope you will miss us too. On the other hand, perhaps this will be a welcome opportunity for you to have a restful retirement in comfortable surroundings. Your life, we know, has had its tragedies and it is something you deserve.

We shall keep you informed about the progress of the scheme and let you know as soon as we can exactly when your relocation will be taking place.

May the Lord bless you.

Nathan Goldfarb (Hon. Sec.)

'Thank you very much,' says Hershel aloud as he reaches the salutation and imagines Nathan Goldfarb (Hon. Sec.) – may curses rain on his hypocrisy – penning it with a sanctimonious smile above his neatly trimmed beard. Final arrangements? Sadly missed? Is he dead already? Has the Burial Society been and gone without Hershel noticing? Was that a taste of his long-awaited Afterlife – a fancy spread in a five star hotel in such elevated company? 'Thanks for nothing.'

He intended to ignore the letter, burn it even, for a pisher like Goldfarb doesn't deserve the effort of a reply. But now he is driven by a passion he suspects has very little to do with his future residence. He is trembling from this passion – wants to scream, to plead with the Almighty, with someone, anyone, not to test Hershel Fine any further, to leave him in peace the way he was left for forty years…

Instead he sighs and, after several moments of thought, begins to write:

Dear Mr Goldfarb,

I see it has come to pass that once again the Children of Israel, who were spared to prosper in the land of plenty, have begun to worship idols. This time, however, they aren't turning their back on Moses, no indeed. This time they are putting him in a glass case safely out of reach, and charging the world to see how quaint he is.

What a good idea, Mr Goldfarb, and how economical. Kills two birds with one stone, as the saying goes. What a pity that the caretaker has to get caught in the crossfire. But lucky for you he's expendable. An old hand at being made homeless. A wandering Jew.

In fact, Mr Goldfarb, I must offer you another solution to the Hershel Fine problem, if that's what it is. Never mind an old age home – another drain on your finances, what for? Why don't you suggest to your Trustees (may they be trustworthy) that they put him on display as a living testimony to the past. A relic. A memory. One of those 'walkie-talkie' exhibits that children love so much.

One more thing, Mr Goldfarb. My thanks to you and the Board for the kind invitation to attend last night's glamorous affair. Such a treat for a caretaker – and such an opportunity to meet new friends and old

Hershel stops writing. He puts down his pen. What is he doing, wasting his words, his irony, his patience on this idiot who is certain to miss the point? Next thing there will be a contract in the post offering minimum terms for Hershel-the-living-relic to be put on show – or, worse, another summons to a party. It will be like when he sent an answer to one of the many research students requesting data on the long-term effects of wartime incarceration on his physical and mental functioning. 'Just put it in your records,' he replied, 'that Hershel Fine is a madman with a broken heart.' A fortnight later came an offer of long-term psychiatric help and a cardiovascular examination.

Not that Hershel has anything against students or psychiatrists, God help them, or the alleviation of heart disease. Or even museums, if that's what people need to feel connected to the past. But for him there's no need to create any more connections. He is already chained to it – it's like a weight that continually threatens to pull him down. And it's the reason why he has pared his present – tried to limit his exposure to any stimuli that might arouse nostalgia. Until last night…

A charity dinner in the West End of London he might have expected to be dull. Tedious, at worst. He thought he might come home with indigestion, a touch of nausea maybe. But no – his stomach, miraculously, remained perfectly settled (thanks maybe to his caution with the fancy food). It was his head and his heart that were afflicted. If only there had been some way to have guarded against the wave of longing and loss that, even now, will not let him be.

When he caught sight of Arnost it all came rushing back.

6.

At the time Hershel hardly noticed the arrival of their twelve-year-old boarder, for his mind was filled with much bigger issues. Why *had* God created the world? Surely not simply for man to serve Him? If so, why should a Supreme Being need the service of mere man? It was all a puzzle – life, death. Especially death.

For several weeks Hershel had been haunted by the knowledge – it had struck him one day like a paralysing blow – that he was inevitably, to die. And then? *Then*? How certain was The World to Come? According to Maimonides, the mind would continue to exist at the highest level to which the soul had been educated. The body, though – no one disputed the fact that it was surely to rot. And if the dead person didn't know absolutely that he was dead, wouldn't he feel the confinement of the grave, the dark and the voracious worms? Why did one have to die, anyway? Surely Adam's sin didn't warrant eternal punishment for all subsequent generations?

On the other hand, Maimonides said that neither death, suffering nor darkness existed. Not in the accepted sense. Since God had created light, it was His right to take it away, which meant that darkness was the temporary absence of light. In the same way, He'd created life and when He took it back...

'Hershel, you're late again,' his mother called as he opened the door. 'We had to start supper without you.'

'I'm sorry,' he said vaguely, still deep in thought.

Was life, then, just the temporary absence of death – or was it the other way round? He would talk to Rachel about it. After supper the two of them would sit together and he would describe the Talmudic passage he had studied that day. It was amazing the way his sister would grasp the most complex ideas and reduce them to their logical core. Did anyone, other than Hershel, have any idea how clever she was?

He washed his hands, praying reflexively, his mind lingering still on matters far removed from the prosaic fact that the meal had begun. And even further removed from the fact that today the boy from Nyirbátor had arrived.

'It's ridiculous how you lose your sense of time.'

His mother's tone cut through his preoccupation. She usually tolerated his absent-mindedness, made fond allowances for his lack of punctuality. What could one do, she would ask indulgently, with a son so bent on learning, one who had undoubtedly inherited his intelligence from generations of erudite forebears? This evening, though, she sounded as though she was angry – and meant it.

'I'm sorry,' he said again, reaching the kitchen and breathing in the smell of roast chicken. Ah – her chicken, she *knew* how much Hershel loved her chicken. Eagerly he stepped into the room.

Afterwards, contemplating that moment and how inconsequential it had seemed, he would wonder at the irony. Who would have thought that while he'd been musing so loftily on Life and Death, there – sitting at his table, eating his mother's food – was Destiny?

But what had he imagined – that Destiny would be silly enough to announce herself? That she would carry a burning torch or a red warning triangle? Oh no. Not Destiny. There she was in perfect camouflage: disguised as a skinny boy with darting eyes and an innocent smile.

While Hershel failed to identify Destiny, he noticed that his mother wore her Sabbath clothes (on a Monday!) and was bending attentively over a strange boy. Then he remembered: the boy, the lodger – of course. It had slipped his mind. Hershel began to say hello, expecting his mother to turn to him with her usual welcome. But no. She seemed engrossed in the boy, watching with concern as he drew each forkful of food to his mouth, with relief and pleasure as he swallowed it. And all the while the boy was gazing at Hershel.

Who sighed. A long, deep, involuntary sigh that came upon him unawares.

'This is Arnost,' his mother said.

Hershel nodded, glancing from the boy to Rachel, sitting opposite him. She, too, was well dressed for a weekday. She looked clean, scrubbed, shiny.

'Arnost arrived from Nyirbátor,' she announced with excitement.

'I see that.'

It occurred to Hershel that this meant his room had been occupied and, for a moment, he regretted the impulse that had made him agree to this measure. But they needed the money, and where else could they have put a paying guest? Swallowing his reluctance, Hershel had offered to vacate his room and move to the kitchen.

'I had to leave some books – only a few of them – in the room,' his mother was saying. 'I wish you'd been here to help. You said you would. You might have found somewhere to store them. I didn't know what to do.'

She spoke querulously but looked at him helplessly, and he saw how difficult this was for her – the effort it took to cope with another new situation. There had been his father's sudden death and Rachel's chronic ill-health. Now a stranger was in their midst needing food and care. Hershel suppressed his resentment. He's a child, he told himself. Merely a child. He smiled at the boy in a kindly way. 'I'm sure you won't mind a few Hebrew books for company.'

The boy returned his gaze, but his face remained expressionless. 'I don't read Hebrew. I'm having a secular education. I'm starting at the Gymnasium tomorrow.'

'I see.' Hershel nodded. If that's what he wanted, who was arguing? 'I hope it all goes well.'

Yetta was clearing the plates, clattering and fussing. 'Did you have enough, Arnost? Rachel, bring him some stewed apple. Do you like stewed apple? Hershel's fond of it too.'

'Sit for a minute, mother,' Hershel urged. 'Relax. Eat your supper – what's the rush?'

'Relax?' She glared at him. 'That's easy for you to say, coming home when all the work's been done.'

'All right, all right,' he soothed. 'I'm sorry. Here – let me help.'

He rose from the table and the boy jumped up too. Eager to please – almost too eager to please. Rachel meanwhile cleared the plates in silence. She had eaten hardly anything, nor had she uttered more than a few politenesses.

'We have things to talk about,' Hershel murmured to her in passing. 'So much to discuss…'

'Rachel has to help *me* this evening,' interrupted Yetta.

'I see,' said Hershel. But he didn't. Was it necessary to change things like this, all for a small boy? Couldn't they have managed without this – found another way to make ends meet? Surely, if Hershel found a job, reduced the hours he spent studying...

He would think about it, speak to her about it. The lodger was maybe a mistake.

But he didn't say anything. He said nothing, did nothing, for – in truth – he was reluctant to relinquish his studies. He didn't want to be employed in a menial job, for in those days he still believed that if he were single-minded he could reach into the heart of something vital, he could even alter the course of human thinking.

How sad he'd have been if he had known the futility of his quest.

Even now, more than sixty years later and with the added potency of hindsight, it makes Hershel want to weep. Would his teachers, his rabbis, those who predicted great things from his Golden Head have ever imagined that this was how it would end? Never mind *end* – the end isn't here yet. It's likely to happen in an establishment for Jewish Seniors. A reputable place, at any rate.

How tragic – and, at the same time, how funny. If he didn't know better Hershel would be bitter with regret. Yet somehow that is contrary to his nature. All he can do is hold on to the fact of his survival: despite all the adversities, here he is – still able to think and reason and remember. That isn't too bad, is it? He tries to imagine how differently things might have turned out if he had tried to tamper with his destiny. What if, for instance, he convinced his mother that Arnost should find another lodging-house... and relinquished his studies, learnt a trade, sent Rachel to school?

If, if, if.

Idle speculation. There are inside forces and outside forces. The inner ones they call self-determination, which offer at least the illusion of control. With outside forces, though – wars, pestilence, Acts of God – it is impossible even to pretend that destiny can be manipulated. All in all, it wouldn't have helped whatever young Hershel tried to do. On the other hand…

He gets up and paces from end to end of his sitting room, now thoroughly agitated despite his protestations of passivity. Live and let live. Die and let die. Live. Die. Live…

No, he cannot forget, he cannot quite forgive. He *will* not – why should he? Is anything more important to him than the memories he cherishes, his links, his continuity? He has sweetened them over the years and allowed sentimentality to creep in, why not? Rachel has gained better health and greater beauty, his mother wisdom, his childhood bliss beyond belief. Hershel would gladly (maybe not gladly, but with a certain composure) have gone to the grave with his recollections intact if that face hadn't returned to haunt him and taunt him.

So now here he is. He should be reading or catching up with his correspondence or seeing to the synagogue (God forbid a thief should break in, where would they all be then?). Instead he is torturing himself with what could have, should have, might have happened more than half a century ago.

Perhaps if it had remained a normal business arrangement, things wouldn't have turned out the way they did. Another useless 'perhaps'. Nevertheless, the original intention was simple, straightforward: the Fines needed money and young Arnost needed a place to stay. Demand and supply. Cause and effect. Logical in the marketplace but complex when human nature interferes.

There was the strain on Yetta, for a start. She was neither stupid nor inadequate – just tired. Her life was tiring, particularly with the addition of another dependent. Even with the lodger she had to supplement their income with the sewing she took in from wealthier neighbours. 'It's my pleasure, my privilege,' she always insisted when Hershel expressed concern about her strained eyes and bleeding fingers. 'What is more important for me than to enable you to study?'

'One day,' Hershel would promise, 'things will be different.'

'Yes.' She sighed. 'Rachel will be married, if we can find her a dowry… and you'll be a famous rabbi. One day things will be very different…'

In the meantime life remained as hard as ever. Even harder, when it turned out that the boarder was no longer paying his way. Hershel discovered this one night when he arrived home very late from the Study House.

He entered the house quietly, shoes in his hand to avoid awakening anyone for he believed that all were asleep. Then he noticed a light, heard movements in his mother's room and called out softly.

'Hush!' She appeared looking exhausted and dishevelled. 'Don't make such a noise.'

'Me? A noise?' he demanded, offended – justifiably so, after all his efforts to be silent. 'Why are you awake at this hour?' He looked past her shoulder through her half-open door and into her room where garments were heaped for mending. Huge piles, impossible quantities. 'Where's Rachel?'

'Asleep. She was too tired – couldn't manage any more. I told her to go to bed.'

'And you – you're tired too.'

'I need to finish. It's for tomorrow.'

'Can't they wait?'

'No, they can't – they won't. Anyway, we need the money. Badly.'

After much pressing on his part and hesitation on hers, it emerged that Arnost's mother had stopped paying rent at least three months before. Simply ceased, without word or warning. Yetta had tried to contact her, to impress upon her that unless the rental was paid Arnost would have to leave. Her letters had been returned unopened. What was she meant to do now – put the child on the street?

'We can't do that,' Hershel said, immediately aware of his ethical duty but conscious, too, of a wave of hostility towards the boy who was causing such strain. 'But why didn't you tell me? We could have talked about it – tried to work something out.'

She pressed her hands on her brow. 'We thought we could manage –

me and Rachel. She insisted that we keep it a secret from you because we want you to carry on studying. We haven't told the boy either because... well, what would be the point?'

Hershel took her arm and gently guided her to a chair.

'You *must* keep up with your studies, Hershel,' she said, looking up at him with tear-filled eyes. 'I promised your father. It was something he always wanted for you.'

He shook his head. 'How can I study while you work yourself to the bone? And Rachel – we know how frail she is, how ill she can get. I can't watch this happening. Tomorrow I'll start looking for a job.'

There was a long silence. 'You can't – you mustn't,' said Yetta at last. 'I don't think I could bear for you to give up your dream... your father's dream. It's important, the most important thing. I hate to do it, Hershel, but we have no choice – Arnost will have to go back to his mother. I'll take him there myself and make sure she is there to receive him. If not... he's a resourceful boy – I'm sure he'll be all right.' She wiped her eyes and stood up resolutely.

For a moment Hershel wavered, for it was an answer – of sorts. His studies were important and – she was right – young Arnost was resourceful. He clearly knew how to get his way, to make his way. It was tempting. Very tempting. And yet... his conscience wouldn't allow it. Hershel guessed from some of the remarks Arnost had made, from the wistful way he sometimes gazed at Yetta, that all was not well between the boy and his mother. He would suffer if he were sent home. 'We can't,' he said. 'We can't do it.'

'We must. What else do you suggest?'

'I don't know – I'll think of something. I could get part-time work, maybe – run messages, serve in a store. Arnost too, when he is older. But we can't send him away. It would be wrong. Father,' he added, using a weapon he knew she couldn't resist, 'would agree with me.'

So Arnost remained and Hershel, having saved him, acquired a kind of responsibility for him. He felt obliged to protect him despite the boy's defiant protestations that he knew quite well how to look out for himself.

Maybe he did. Who was Hershel to argue? He could only advise, watch, guide, discuss – and observe that although young Arnost would strut like a peacock down the streets of Nyíregháza there was something acutely lonely about him.

One night – a night Hershel would never forget – he glimpsed Arnost's troubled soul. It was late. Yetta and Rachel were in bed and Hershel had returned home from the House of Study to find the boy in the kitchen concentrating intently on something he was cradling on his lap. Hershel watched, unobserved. Arnost didn't stir, even when Hershel coughed discreetly to alert him to his presence.

Then he noticed that the boy's cheeks were wet with tears and that the object of his attention and evident grief was a small creature, a tiny yellow... could it be a *chicken*? 'It's no good,' Arnost was muttering through clenched teeth. 'She's dead. Quite dead...' Looking up, he saw Hershel and shook his head miserably.

Hershel, stunned by the revelation that this self-sufficient braggart had the capacity to adopt a pet and lament its passing, reached forward and touched Arnost's shoulder. 'I'm sorry,' he managed, half-expecting the gesture to be met with one of Arnost's characteristically surly rebuffs. But the boy accepted his solace without hiding his distress. He looked small and hopeless.

'I looked after a baby chick once,' Hershel ventured. 'It also died. What can one do?'

Arnost didn't respond.

'We can find you another one,' Hershel went on encouragingly. 'Tomorrow morning early I'll speak to my mother.'

'It's not *this* thing – I don't care about it one bit,' said Arnold, looking away. 'Stupid animal! It was only fit for eating anyway.'

'What then? Why are you so upset?' Gently, carefully, Hershel sat down beside Arnost and in sobbing bursts the boy told him about the loss of his mother and how, after all this time, he still longed for a particular chicken he'd named Julis. And how, hard as he tried, he could no longer picture them clearly – neither his mother nor his beloved chick.

Hershel was stunned by the force of Arnost's despair. His impulse was to honour this display of frustrated misery with his own revelation of angry impotence in the face of great loss. He began to lean towards Arnost and for a moment their eyes locked in mutual empathy. But something stopped Hershel, forced him to turn away. He had never properly confronted the raw grief that still festered after the death of his father, the fury that sometimes raged within him at the weight of responsibility that had been thrust upon him. It was too frightening – too exhausting. He shut his eyes, clenched his fists and heard himself mumbling about his blessed belief in the Holy Texts and his profound sense of the importance of venerating memory.

'We are the past,' he said, aware of the portentousness of his words, the sonority of his tone, but unable to stop himself. 'Singly and collectively, we are our past and should cherish the good with the bad. If you like, Arnost, I'll show you some of the writings – you may find them comforting. I'm sure you will...'

Arnost looked at him in momentary bewilderment. Then, as though a curtain had dropped over his vulnerability, the familiar scornful expression returned to his face. 'How do *you* know what will comfort me?' he asked – and suddenly he was no longer a defenceless child. Hershel recoiled. 'You don't know me at all. Do you think I want to have anything to do with your ridiculous texts? Do you really imagine I want to be like *you*?' His tears had dried. With composure he stood up to dispose of the feathery remains. 'Goodnight,' he said curtly to Hershel and disappeared.

Hershel sat thinking long after the stove had grown cold. His anger at Arnost's rebuff subsided with the dying flames and left him with a sense of loss quite unlike the grief for his father and inexplicable in terms of Talmudic teachings. The boy was arrogant and impossible, but even so Hershel was aware that he had failed.

The incident was never referred to again. Hershel immersed himself in his studies while Arnost, having apparently conquered his demons, focused his energies on his schoolwork and his rapidly increasing stature. He studied himself minutely in the mirror, examining his face and measuring his height. One day he announced with great relish that, despite Hershel's seniority, Arnost was now the taller of the two.

Yetta endorsed his self-satisfaction, which irritated Hershel. 'Isn't he turning into a fine looking boy?' she would remark, fondly ruffling his hair. Hershel wondered whether she had forgotten her decision to send him back home and Hershel's intervention to prevent this. She took full credit for the fine creature she had housed and fed and watered.

Arnost was now clearly an expert in the concealment and denial of his vulnerability. He had ceased to acknowledge Hershel's attempts to be kind. He seemed to prefer not to acknowledge Hershel at all. Worse – he used every opportunity he found to pour scorn on Jewish traditions, as represented by Hershel. He would proclaim disdainfully how Hershel was 'so *obviously* a Jew'. In the street with his friends from the Gymnasium, he would deliberately walk on if Hershel passed, as though denying his existence.

It was a phase, decided Hershel – for that was easier than mulling over his missed opportunity to forge a bond with the boy. Instead he rationalised the rejection as a necessary step in Arnost's development. What else did he have to rebel against? How else would he establish his identity? He'd come round – he would mellow. Everyone did eventually. After all, it wasn't as though Hershel needed Arnost's approval.

If only Yetta felt this way. It irked Hershel to observe his mother succumbing to Arnost's maturing charm. Even more irritating was the way Rachel had started behaving in his company – giggling, flirting, simpering coquettishly. Hershel kept searching in vain for traces of his soulmate and intellectual companion. 'Be careful,' he wanted to say to his mother and sister, but knew they would laugh off his warning as mere jealousy. Which it probably was, for he had no evidence of ill intent on Arnost's part at all.

So he kept silent. He engrossed himself in his studies and sadly remembered the nights he and Rachel had explored Biblical passages together. He recalled how she had revealed some of the answers even his most learned teachers had missed. How she had changed.

But everything changed. The seasons, the climate, the most stable economies. They changed and changed again – the only certainty being that summer would return. He would wait for summer. He'd sit tight and trust the inevitability of summer's return.

Is that faith, Hershel wonders? Is faith the acceptance that all things are transient – that human life, like the seasons, will inevitably bud and flower and fall? Is this trust in some ultimate continuity the most one can achieve?

Hershel has few material possessions, no family and maybe a couple of friends. His life has been devoted to studying, to straining after truths. He has seen the futility of putting store by things or places or even people. He believes that – at least – he has mastered faith.

Then why, after all, is he so deeply disturbed by a glimpse of someone from the past? He should be able to dismiss it, forget it – doesn't he have troubles enough without it? Who needs Arnost Rosenbaum (or whatever he now calls himself) to haunt him again at this point in his life? He's history. Hershel has already wasted enough time railing against him, the murderer, the thief.

'That's it,' he says aloud, resolutely. He'll get on with his chores – there's plenty to be done. First a cup of tea maybe, with something to eat. A soft-boiled egg would be perfect. There is something reliable and comforting about a soft-boiled egg. In fact, if he should turn out to be institutionalised he'll make sure there are no restrictions on soft-boiled eggs.

Hershel slowly, groaningly, rises to his feet and shuffles across the floor to fill the kettle. As he turns it on, there is a knock on the door.

'Who is it?' he calls, slightly annoyed. Company he doesn't need. There is more than enough company in his head.

'I'm sorry to disturb you, Mr Fine...' A woman's voice. Familiar. He opens the door.

'Oh – good morning,' he says, recognising that busybody Lily What's-her-name from last night. What is she doing here with that pitying look on her face? Losing his flat is unfortunate, seeing Arnost again is a curse. But compassion from a do-gooder – *that* he needs like a hole in the head.

7.

Lily sees the kettle almost the instant she walks through the door. 'Mr Fine,' she exclaims, 'You were about to have tea! Don't let me stop you.'

'It doesn't matter,' he begins – then sees she is looking at him with bright eager eyes. 'Maybe you want to join me?' he offers reluctantly.

'That would be *lovely*. Just what I need. I can't tell you what sort of a morning it has been so far. By the way, I must apologise for intruding like this…'

'It doesn't matter,' he repeats unenthusiastically. Suddenly he's off the idea of tea – an egg he can't even think about. How long will she stay here, the busybody? With a little luck she's on her way somewhere else, just passing by?

But no. 'I came to see you *specially*,' she says, bustling about, shedding her coat and scarf and cardigan. She urges him to take a seat while she makes the tea. She washes the cups, rinses the dishcloth then sniffs it doubtfully before spreading it out to dry. Stop, stop, Hershel wants to say. What right do you have? Who invited you here? But he doesn't open his mouth. He sits there, speechlessly trying to compose himself.

'Milk? Sugar?' she asks.

'Both,' he manages.

'So here we are,' she trills, placing his cup and hers on the table and drawing up a chair. 'Now we can talk.'

He takes a long, noisy sip of tea – intentionally signalling his antisocial disposition. But Lily takes no notice. She is rummaging in her handbag and eventually pulls out a notebook and a pen. 'Right,' she says, 'let's get on with it.'

'With what?' he asks, puzzled.

'Mr Fine… can I call you Hershel?'

'Of course.' She can call him what she wants, only leave him in peace.

'The thing is,' she says earnestly, 'I have taken it upon myself to help you.'

'Oh?'

'After meeting you last night I decided I couldn't live with myself unless I did something positive about this... this *iniquity.*' She exhales loudly and defiantly and Hershel – who has managed to avoid close contact with do-gooders until now – is suddenly anxious about the state of her respiration. 'So,' she continues, breathing more normally thank goodness, 'we have to get on with the petition.'

'The petition? What petition? Mrs Sanderson...'

'Lily – please.'

'I'm not really the sort of person to make a big noise about something...'

'That's *exactly* why I'm so keen to help. It's what I was saying on the phone to Helena earlier – they're taking advantage of you. If you *were* the sort to make a fuss, no one would risk the scandal.'

'A scandal?' It's unpleasant to face the possibility of being forced to move. Nasty – maybe even ruthless. But a scandal? 'That, if you don't mind my saying so, is an overstatement. Listen, Lily – I appreciate your sympathy, but I think I'll manage somehow. And, between us, if one has to go to a home ... worse can happen, I assure you. Much worse.'

She is stubborn though. Like a mule. 'But last night,' she protests, 'you told me you were furious – you'd trusted the synagogue committee and it had let you down.'

'I changed my mind.' What should he tell her – that during the course of the evening he'd caught sight of Arnost and how much it disturbed him? That he now prefers to hide in his flat and submit to his fate than to avoid a repetition of the distress that the single glimpse aroused? Can someone like Lily comprehend something like that? Never. She'll pester him with questions about how, when and where he knew Arnost. She wants a scandal? Hershel can give her a scandal or two – but he won't. All he wants is for her to swallow her tea and leave. 'I want you to forget the whole thing,' he says with an air of finality.

There is a short silence.

'Well,' she says thoughtfully – and for an instant Hershel believes he has won. 'I can understand – I truly can – your reluctance to be in the public eye. So perhaps the petition isn't a good idea. But that's a side issue, something that came up only this morning. The most *important* thing – and this is why I'm here – is to get all the facts straight for my presentation to the Trustees.'

So now it's a presentation. 'Lily,' he says wearily, 'didn't you hear what I said?'

'It won't involve you at all, I swear on my life. You'll simply give me the information I need, and the next time you hear from me it will be with good news.'

'I told you – it doesn't matter any more.'

'But it's not only *you* we're talking about. It's the principle. If you let them tread roughshod over you, they'll bully someone else. I'm committed to this, Hershel – I can't let go.'

She looks so passionate, so tragic, that Hershel finds himself moved by her plight. He wonders briefly whether there's a cause with more universal resonance to which she can attach ardour of this magnitude, but so grave is her demeanour, so fervent her gaze, that he doesn't have the heart to resist any longer. 'All right.' He sighs deeply. 'What is it you want to know?'

Two hours later, Lily is on the telephone to Helena. She has completed her interview and tidied Hershel's flat and left him in a state of stunned capitulation, his lap piled with glossy material promoting her favourite good causes.

'Helena, he's too sweet for words.'

'Who?'

'The caretaker – Hershel – we're absolutely the best of friends.'

'What are you talking about, Lily?'

'I was at his flat first thing this morning. Didn't I swear to you that I wasn't going to let the matter rest?'

'Oh, Lily – *honestly…*'

'Anyway, he finally agreed that I should put his case before the Board and we had a long chat. I do think the poor man is terribly depressed – but then, who wouldn't be with the sort of life he's had? I think I'm going to try and convince him to join the Survivor Centre when all this is over… Oh, and listen to this Helena – he's from Hungary. As I got home it occurred to me... isn't that where Arnold came from?'

'Well, *originally...*'

'I must tell Hershel about him. Who knows? Maybe they'll find something in common. I didn't want to press too hard with Hershel today – he seemed quite closed... some sort of therapy would definitely do him good... he lost his entire family, I gathered. Everyone.'

'How sad. Lily, can we talk about this later? I have a hair appointment.'

'I think we should bring them together.'

'Who? Lily, I'm running late.'

'Hershel and Arnold.'

'Hershel and *Arnold*? *My* Arnold?'

'Don't you think it's a brilliant idea? I know Arnold doesn't usually involve himself in this sort of thing – but maybe now that he's retired?'

'I can't imagine he'd agree. What would be the point?'

'The point? Oh, Helena – sometimes you're so slow. The other day we were talking about events to launch the museum. This would be perfect: an open discussion led by two men who survived God-knows-what in Europe and made new lives in England. Perhaps we can get the rabbi or someone to moderate. Now tell me: is it or is it not a brainwave?'

'It's not bad, Lily – but can we discuss it later – I *really...*'

'Have a word with Arnold, though.'

'I can't see him agreeing, but I'll try.'

She broaches the subject that evening. Arnold has returned from a successful session of bridge in a particularly genial frame of mind. 'We had the most fascinating hands,' he enthuses. 'Tell me, Helena – what would you bid with five diamonds headed by a nine, three small hearts, the king and queen of spades and the ace, king, queen of clubs?'

'A diamond?'

He bangs his palm exultantly on the table. 'Well can you believe that Lionel called a heart? But do you know what I did – with sixteen points and spades – I thought the hell with it and took a chance and went straight to six spades. And what do you think happened?'

'What?' says Helena, playing along.

'I made it.'

'Excellent. Well done.' Changing her tone, she embarks on Lily's request: 'Arnold, I've had Lily Sanderson on at me all day…'

'Lily Sanderson,' he interrupts scornfully. 'What is she fussing about now?'

'She has a bee in her bonnet…'

'May it sting her in the ear.'

'Don't be mean. She's very good-natured. It's amazing the way she has taken the case of this old caretaker to heart. She's like that though – an enthusiast. An asset to any committee, so long as she's kept under control. You won't believe what she did this morning without consulting a soul?'

'What?' he asks reluctantly, for he has a hunch about where this conversation is heading.

'She went off to see the old man – to visit him in his flat. He's an angel, she says. A real pet. Comes from Hungary too, apparently. His name's Hershel Fine. Does that ring a bell?'

'Helena, for God's sake – it's like saying someone comes from Paris or New York and assuming…'

'Of course, of course. I told Lily it was highly unlikely. There must be thousands of Hungarians in London – and anyway I'm sure his background is completely different to yours. Lily's impossible, though, when she gets something into her head. She insisted that I speak to you about this romantic notion she has about getting the two of you together.'

'*What*?' He turns away from her to hide his agitation. The interfering witch – how dare she? 'What are you talking about?'

Helena gives one of her light little laughs and launches herself into her nocturnal skin care routine. 'I know – it is rather silly,' she says. 'You'll probably loathe each other on sight and the whole thing will be a complete disaster.'

'Helena,' he breaks in – so sharply that she suspends her night cream application and stares at him curiously. 'I'm telling you here and now – I have no interest at *all* in meeting a synagogue caretaker. None. Tell Lily

Sanderson she can forget it.'

'Oh, all right then,' she concedes, clearly taken aback by his vehemence. She laughs again, this time slightly nervously. 'If that's the way you feel, I hate to tell you about the other scheme she's cooking up.'

'What's that?'

'She's hoping to get the two of you to take part in one of our museum launch events. A platform discussion or something.' Her voice tails off as she observes the horror with which he is regarding her. 'Of course, it's entirely up to you. I pointed out to Lily that you weren't really the sort to talk about personal things in public – but she insisted that I mention it anyway. One never knew, she said. People change.'

'Very well,' he says in a way that doesn't sound very well. 'You've mentioned it. I don't want to hear about it again.' He turns away, heading for the bathroom – for ablution, medication, bed, sleep.

Helena resumes her face massage with vigour, concentrating on the delicate tissue around her eyes. 'Arnold,' she calls after a while. 'Please – one second – one final thing before we drop the subject.'

'What?' he asks crossly, reappearing at the door.

'The thing about Lily is that once she's set her heart on something she gets stubborn. What I'm saying is that she doesn't easily take *no* as an answer.'

'You'll have to convince her then. I mean it, Helena – I really do. I want to have nothing – nothing *whatsoever* – to do with the whole thing.'

'Yes – yes, I know. I understand. I was just thinking, though, that maybe she'd accept it better coming from you. Why don't you have a word with her tomorrow evening when she comes over for the Board Meeting? Quietly, firmly.'

'I know how to deal with Lily Sanderson, thank you.'

'You'll talk to her then?'

He returns to the bathroom without saying another word.

8.

MINUTES OF THE FIFTH MEETING OF THE BOARD OF TRUSTEES FOR THE MUSEUM OF JEWISH LIFE

18TH APRIL AT 8.30PM

VENUE: THE HOME OF MRS HELENA ROSE

Present: Helena Rose (Chair)
Frank Singer
Lily Sanderson
Edward King
Jeremy Harris (Honorary Treasurer)
Betty Wilson (Honorary Secretary)
Guest: Bernard Kaplan

Our Chair, Helena Rose, opened the proceedings with a vote of thanks to all concerned for the success of the recent dinner to boost the Museum Fund. Betty Wilson then proposed a very hearty vote of thanks to the Chair herself for the inspirational way she had led her band of devoted workers thus far and the excellent speech she had made. Lily Sanderson seconded the proposal which was enthusiastically and unanimously accepted.

The Treasurer, Jeremy Harris, was called on to give an account of the financial state of the Fund, which he described as 'solid'. He invited Trustees to examine the balance sheet and it was unanimously agreed that although there seemed no reason for anxiety at present, complacency would be dangerous and the impetus of the fund-raising programme should be sustained.

Frank Singer, who has been liasing with the Architects and the Planning Committee, gave a report on the Building Programme, and was pleased to announce that it was proceeding according to schedule. Construction of the museum building is well under way and Trustees will soon be invited to a Site Inspection. As far as the synagogue proper is concerned, Mr Singer said work would soon begin on rewiring, repointing and general renovation.

Edward King wondered what plans had been made to make the

synagogue more visitor-friendly and suggested a Refreshment Area specialising in traditional Jewish foods, as well as a series of Sound and Light Shows to mark Festivals. Frank Singer, however, felt that it should be left intact as a Real Working Synagogue. He said he had recently visited a Coal-Mining Museum in a defunct Staffordshire mine, where visitors were taken underground as a 'living experience'. He believed the synagogue should be operated along those lines.

Moving on to Other Matters, the Chair mentioned the particular interest of Mr Bernard Kaplan (the new Cantor) in the installation of computer technology in the Museum – which was why he had been invited to the meeting. Mr Kaplan agreed to produce a report on the establishment of an Internet Site devoted to Heritage Appreciation. There was enthusiasm from the Trustees and animated discussion until the Chair called the meeting to order.

She was about to close the meeting when Lily Sanderson raised an Additional Matter: the Synagogue Caretaker. Apparently the Caretaker is to be re-housed in order to make way for a curator. Mrs Sanderson felt this should be opposed by the Trustees on Humanitarian Grounds. It was pointed out that the Caretaker's employment was the responsibility of the Synagogue Board and not the Museum Trustees. Mrs Sanderson was insistent that the matter be investigated. She presented an Appeal she had drawn up on the Caretaker's behalf. Betty Wilson proposed that a letter of objection be sent to the Synagogue Board and volunteered to draft it.

Lily Sanderson brought up yet another Additional Matter: the programme of events to launch the Museum. Trustees felt that discussion on this Matter should be postponed for a future meeting, but Mrs Sanderson insisted that a Launch Co-ordinator be immediately appointed. Announcing she had some innovative ideas, she volunteered for the position. A vote was taken and she was elected by three votes to one (the Chair and Hon Sec abstained). Mrs Sanderson thanked the Trustees for this show of confidence in her and announced she would set up an Events Sub-Committee.

There being no further business, the meeting terminated at 10.05pm. Coffee and cakes were served.

Signed,

Mrs Betty Wilson (Honorary Secretary).

9.

Coffee and cakes are still being ingested when Arnold returns home. He opens the door quietly and, hearing with dismay the cup-clinking clamour, tries to sneak upstairs. But Lily Sanderson spots him.

'Arnold!' she shrieks. 'Just the person I was hoping to see!'

'Good evening.' He tries to look moderately pleased – which he isn't, since the reason he endured a tasteless meal and tedious conversation in his Mayfair club was specifically to avoid Lily and her mob. He smiles. 'I hope you had a successful meeting,' he murmurs, edging towards the staircase.

'Excellent.' She applies a restraining hand to his arm. 'Please don't run away. There's something I must talk to you about.'

'Perhaps another time.' He proceeds resolutely and almost achieves an exit when Betty Wilson joins the siege.

'Your ears must have been burning, Arnold,' she cries.

'Yes,' Lily agrees, rounding on him with glee. 'I was just remarking to Betty what a coincidence it is that you and our darling caretaker come from the same part of the world.'

'As I pointed out to Helena earlier, there are thousands of Hungarians in London,' he says abruptly. Thinking: what would she say if she knew the extent of the coincidence? And: how has Hershel suddenly become her *darling* caretaker? Arnold is suddenly afraid of what Hershel might have confided to her with this new-found intimacy. Perhaps she knows? Nonsense, she can't – being Lily, she would have said. Lily is hardly a model of restraint. Nevertheless, his heart begins to race and his skin to prickle. 'Will you excuse me? We can discuss the matter another time. I need to attend to some urgent business.'

But Lily obstructs his escape route. 'One minute.'

Arnold, who normally takes pride in his self-control, fears this may be a test too far. Suppressing an urge to throttle her, he looks around wildly in search of Helena. Where is she? Surely she can see he's surrounded? Doesn't she know how much he loathes her female friends?

'Let's set a time and place at least,' Lily continues, while Betty smiles and nods at her side.

'Ring me tomorrow, or – better still – arrange it with Helena,' he mutters though clenched jaws. 'If you can find her,' he adds, still scanning the room without success.

He sees Frank Singer guffawing uproariously at a remark by Edward King. The punchline to a dirty joke probably. These people pretend to be cultured but in truth are illiterate. As for that Jeremy Harris sniggering on the side – didn't Arnold explicitly instruct Helena not to have him in the house after that fraud scandal? Arnold can't abide questionable business ethics. He'll speak to her about this; it is in direct opposition to his wishes. Where on earth *is* she?

'Evening, Arnold,' calls Frank Singer as he passes. 'Everything all right?'

'Yes, thank you,' Arnold answers. What does he mean – *everything all right*? Has anyone indicated anything to the contrary? Of course not – it's a mere formality, a platitude. He's becoming paranoid. 'Have you seen Helena?' he asks.

'I think she went off with that Kaplan fellow – the new Cantor,' says Edward King. 'I heard him asking her to show him something or other – her etchings, perhaps? *I*'d go and find them quickly if I were you.' He winks meaningfully while Frank Singer splutters with mirth. Arnold, striding past, gives them both a withering look. He pointedly ignores Jeremy Harris.

'Helena,' he calls from the bottom of the stairs.

After a lengthy silence, her voice floats down. 'I'm here. Upstairs, in the study. Is that you, Arnold?'

He starts climbing, his anger mounting with every step. By the time he reaches the study (it's *his* study – what does she mean: *the* study? Since when has it become a communal space?) he's at breaking point.

'Arnold – it *is* you!' She turns from the desk to face him (*the* desk? *His* desk – his, his, *his*), while behind her, having taken smug occupation of his chair, leers the odious Kaplan. 'Arnold,' he gushes, springing to his feet, eagerly proffering his hand. 'I don't think we've formally met, but someone pointed you out the other evening – and of course Helena's been telling me all about you.'

'I see.' Arnold stands stiff and still in the doorway. He doesn't see why he is suddenly proving such a rich source of conversation. He doesn't see why this bumptious little philanderer should be cavorting upstairs with his wife. And he certainly doesn't see why, under the circumstances, he should be expected to shake the said philanderer's hand. He directs a stern gaze at Helena. 'You seem to have abandoned your guests.'

She laughs uneasily. Arnold sees that her face is flushed and a few wisps of hair have lost their bearings. 'The guests,' she says, 'have been looked after extremely well. I was showing Bernard your new laptop – he's one of those amazingly clever people who actually understands how these things work.'

'It's a wonderful little machine,' enthuses Bernard. 'An amazing capacity for its size.'

'Really?' Arnold's tone makes manifest his lack of interest in the subject. He'd never wanted the computer, which was foisted on him by the family in a futile effort to bring him up to date. Nor does he want this stranger fiddling in his study. 'To me it seems hardly more than a glorified toy.'

'Not at all,' exclaims Helena, sidling up to the silly man and bending over him to watch his fingers fox-trotting on the keyboard, creating a myriad of shapes and colours on the screen. 'If *you* can't see the point of it, I have a good mind to learn how to use it myself. Bernard says we really ought to get online – we'd never look back.'

Arnold, still hovering at the door, clears his throat disparagingly – but the impact is lost in a sequence of electronic bleeps and clicks emanating from this thing that is holding his wife so rapt. Or is it Bernard who's fascinating her? Isn't he meant to be a cantor? Why isn't he warbling in the synagogue instead of meddling with another man's wife? Arnold coughs again, and this time Helena hears it. She turns round sharply, looking annoyed. *Annoyed*? *She* has the gall to look annoyed? 'I'm off to bed,' Arnold announces, heavily emphasising each word. 'Don't you think, Madame Chair, that you have been absent from your meeting long enough?'

'The meeting's over,' she snaps – and then, glancing at Bernard, modifies the unpleasantness of her tone with another small laugh. 'Come along, Bernard – we'd better get downstairs and join the others. You'll have to continue the lesson another time.'

'With the greatest pleasure.' Bernard presses various buttons and closes the computer with a loud double-click. 'There!' He turns to face Arnold, smiling with the kind of radiant innocence that means he is either supremely bad or completely off his head. Arnold despises him either way. Bernard, however, seems impervious to the ill-will and extends his hand for another rebuff. 'Arnold, I'm very glad to have met you.'

Stiffly Arnold moves aside for the pair of them to pass.

'You were extremely rude,' she says later, after the guests have gone and she has joined him in bed.

'Rude?' he repeats, pretending to be engrossed in an elderly tome about German Romanticism that he borrowed from the London Library. Taking out life membership of the library was one of his post-retirement moves – an act of faith in his longevity, he declared to Helena. A vote of confidence in his undiminished intellectual capacity, which he now feels obliged to feed with concentrated profundity – and which he fears (but will never admit) is buckling under the strain. Not buckling, exactly. Weary. Fuzzy. Distracted perhaps by recent events.

'Arnold, stop reading for a moment and listen to me.'

Sighing, he raises his eyes. She wants a confrontation, it seems. He hates scenes and often congratulates himself on the air of tranquillity he has fostered over forty-odd years of marriage. There have been a few minor contretemps from time to time – mostly when Helena was hormonally unstable. Even tonight, despite being provoked almost to the point of violence, he managed to turn the other cheek. But if she insists on combat… 'What would you like to discuss?' he asks icily.

She sits up, drawing breath so intensely that her nostrils flare – and out it comes: his uncalled-for aggression, the arrogance he showed towards a blameless young man who had tried to be nothing but helpful and polite, despite Arnold's irrational hostility. His abruptness with Lily and Betty (it was remarked on – the girls were mystified, *mystified* by his behaviour), and his general ill will. What is the matter with him? Is it his age, his retirement, something physically amiss? Does he have an explanation, any reason at all? If so, she'll try to understand and be tolerant. If not...

'For God's sake!' Arnold interrupts angrily. 'I will not lie here taking this. There's a limit. What do you mean – my hostility, my arrogance? Do you have any idea what a fool you have made of yourself, flirting like that with a man half your age? Are you aware of the ridicule you're subjecting yourself to? Do you realise that you are humiliating your husband? As for Lily and Betty – the sooner they realise that I am not to be included in their interfering plans, the better it will be. Haven't I told you, absolutely and irrevocably, that I will not, under any circumstances, have anything to do with Hershel Fine? Are you deaf?'

She retreats, subdued by the force of his response. Probably quite taken aback, thinks Arnold with grim satisfaction, by the revelation that her quietly spoken husband has the capacity to be roused to such a pitch. Well, it's time she discovers with whom she is dealing. It is time she knows...

An uncomfortable knot forms in his stomach. He swallows hard, for it seems to be pressing upwards to his throat. It is dread. He cannot recall ever feeling such dread.

'Well,' she is saying, no longer belligerent but still distinctly cool, 'I have no idea why you're acting in this peculiar way. All I can say is that I hope you're more like yourself tomorrow. We have the whole family coming for supper – including Evie, would you believe? – and we certainly don't need tension.'

He doesn't respond. Instead, he returns to the mind-numbing erudition of his book and keeps his eyes forcibly focused on the text. At last she turns off her bedside lamp and positions herself for sleep.

10.

Helena's approach to family dinners is that of a military commander heading a complex campaign. She barks orders. She keeps in constant telephonic contact with the butcher, the baker, the greengrocer and various other outposts of her empire. The household, generally, is maintained in a state of red alert. Arnold keeps mainly to his study.

It's providential – he tells himself – that this flurry of activity has arisen to subsume all traces of last night's dissent. Providential too that he is to be given a reminder of his place at the head of the wonderful family that he (and Helena, of course) created. *Paterfamilias*, he thinks, relishing the weight of the word. 'Paterfamilias,' he tries aloud – and the utterance induces such a rush of well being that he braves campaign headquarters to request a cup of coffee.

'In a moment, Arnold,' says Helena distractedly. She is perched on a kitchen stool with the telephone jammed to her ear. 'I must try and get hold of another chicken. I've never come across such scrawny birds as the pair they delivered – they'll *never* feed everyone.'

The idea of chicken suddenly dampens Arnold's mood. 'I'd have preferred lamb tonight,' he says moodily.

'Oh? I thought you liked chicken.' Helena looks at him in surprise. 'Anyway, Martin specially asked for it. He adores my herb-and-breadcrumb stuffing.'

Martin. Arnold's mood dips further as he remembers how much he dislikes his son-in-law and how appalled he was when his second-born, Sandra, brought him home. A crass used-car salesman, for goodness sake. With Sandra's education, breeding and wealth, he'd expected her to do better. 'Are the children coming?' he asks.

'Of course.' Helena's face brightens at the mention of their grandchildren. 'Even William. Sandra's promised to make him rest this afternoon so that he doesn't get over-tired. You know how fractious he can become… Oh, yes – please – tell him it's Mrs Rose calling about the roasting fowl. It's urgent.'

Arnold decides that his coffee will not be forthcoming and that if he makes himself too conspicuous in the kitchen he'll be called upon to help. On the other hand, he can't be expected to spend the entire day skulking in his study without refreshment. The dilemma makes him cross. Grumpily he wanders from the kitchen to the dining room. His spirits recover at the spectacle of the table, opulently set for ten. How beautiful it looks: snow-white linen, sparkling silverware. Tangible evidence of his success.

He tells himself how proud he should be of the way he – a penniless émigré – has acquired so much. Most people need a whole lifetime, generations even, to reach Arnold's level of refinement and elegance. In truth, most of the refugees who came here after the War didn't even allow themselves to dream about such splendour. They let themselves to be beaten into submission and oozed gratitude for any small scrap. Arnold, on the other hand, arrived with his head held high. He respected himself, evoked respect from others, and never doubted that he would make something of himself. And here he is.

Paterfamilias, he thinks yet again as he takes his seat at the head of the table. He runs a proprietary eye from chair to chair which, in his mind, he fills with his progeny. A good-looking lot, he thinks. Good-looking, intelligent, a credit to their father. And their mother, of course.

Simon their first-born, for instance, is an exemplary son. Without a hitch he proceeded from Eton to Cambridge to a full partnership in a law practice. He married along the way as well – managing even that with commendable taste and efficiency. Simon's wife, Louise, is not only beautiful but also a successful lawyer in her own right. And Amy, their ten-year-old, is already showing signs of academic distinction – not to mention her parents' good looks.

Not that Sandra has done badly. Arnold wouldn't choose Martin as a son-in-law, but at least he makes a living. And the two children seem to be taking after their mother rather than their father, thank heaven, although Rebecca isn't turning out to be quite as clever or pretty as her cousin Amy. But this is only to be expected, for Arnold recalls vaguely that Sandra wasn't a brilliant child.

His memories of his children's early years are hazy because Helena was largely responsible for their care. Which is the way things should be. Arnold doesn't approve of Martin's involvement with bottles and nappies and schools. It isn't manly. William will suffer for it eventually. A boy needs a strong role model, as he will tell Martin some day. Not in front of Evie, of course. With her feminist notions, she'd probably hit the roof.

Arnold tenses at the thought of his youngest child. This baffles him, since she has always been his favourite, his particular source of pleasure. They were close, he and Evie. She was livelier, more original, much more interesting than the others. He always assumed that Simon and Sandra – and even Helena – respected and admired him; Evie's esteem he had to work for.

And he achieved it. All through her teens, and even into her twenties, she talked to him and confided in him. Over the years she extracted from him more personal revelations than he risked with anyone else. Of late, though, she seems to have distanced herself from him, no longer seeking his approval – which is only to be expected from someone almost thirty. But Arnold is aware of something else: an edge of hardness that makes him wary in her presence.

Can it be that she's bitter about not yet being married? Perhaps, despite her avowed dedication to her job as a social worker, she isn't properly fulfilled? With her exceptional talents, Arnold hoped she would achieve higher things.

Maybe she needs encouragement, a pep talk. He decides to seat Evie on his left and offer her choice morsels and sensible advice. That will cheer her up.

Yes – all in all, the evening promises to be enjoyable. Everyone will talk and laugh and value one another and feel wonderfully content. Arnold anticipates a perfect family meal.

It starts that way. Or seemingly so, for so determined is Arnold to see his family as flawless that he is blind to the intimations of the disaster to come.

Simon arrives with a bottle of Scotch. Normally it's a bunch of flowers prettily presented by Amy or, on special occasions, a carefully chosen

French wine. Tonight, though, it is Scotch – of which Simon begins to drink without waiting to be offered. 'Excuse me,' he says, pouring himself out a hefty tot, which he swallows in a single gulp. 'There. That feels slightly better.'

'Another?' offers Arnold, taking charge of the bottle and slipping into his habitual role of the genial host. 'There are times when there is nothing like a stiff Scotch.'

'There are times indeed,' says Simon.

Arnold, refilling his son's glass, thinks his tone sounds unusually harsh, but puts this down to end-of-week exhaustion. In a moment the others will get here and everyone will relax. Family news will be amiably exchanged and all will be well.

This is what happens – more or less. Sandra and Martin finally make their noisy entrance with sufficient child-paraphernalia to set up a mobile crèche. Arnold glances at Amy, who is quietly engrossed in a book, and is about to comment favourably on her behaviour. But this would be lost in the clanging of toys, the children's squabbling and Sandra's shrill attempts to restore order.

'Who wants what to drink?' Arnold tries, managing to sustain his geniality. Just. He can't help noticing that the level of Scotch has substantially decreased and deftly removes the bottle from Simon's reach.

'Hang on there,' objects Simon, his voice cutting sharply above the noise. There's an uncomfortable silence until Helena appears and places a calming hand on her son's shoulder.

'Supper,' she announces, 'will be ready in a couple of minutes. Evie just phoned to say she'll be slightly delayed and we should carry on without her.'

'Delayed?' Arnold echoes, now beginning to foresee that the evening may not turn out quite as envisaged.

'Don't worry – she'll be here soon,' Helena soothes. 'In the meantime, why don't we all take our seats in the dining room? Arnold – will you sort everyone out while I attend to the soup?'

Arnold rises to his feet, relieved to have been assigned a task. 'Everyone – please follow me.' But the hubbub continues unabated. No one, it seems, is paying him the slightest attention. 'Will everyone please follow me to the dining room,' he booms – and this time there is a response. They move towards him – all except William, who remains on the floor with his toys in stolid defiance.

'Come along, William,' coaxes Sandra. 'Let's go and see what delicious food Grandma has prepared for us. You know how we all love Grandma's food.'

'Don't want Grandma's food – I *hate* Grandma's food – I want to play with my toys.'

'William,' pleads Sandra.

'Won't! Won't! Won't!' William yells. Sandra looks helpless. Martin bends down and tries to reason with the boy. Reasoning with a two-year-old, for God's sake, thinks Arnold. He watches in disbelief for a moment or two and then explodes: 'The child needs discipline – a sharp smack, not a debate. William! To the dining room! Immediately!'

William gazes at his grandfather with wide, shocked eyes and quietly obeys.

'So. Here we are,' says Arnold in some triumph when the family has finally assembled. There is an empty seat on his left, but Helena has assured them that Evie will arrive soon. A minor motor breakdown is the explanation for her delay. This is perfectly acceptable. Arnold gazes round the table, beaming, and tries to ignore the fact that Simon, for one, isn't smiling back. His daughter-in-law Louise, he notices, is dressed as beautifully as ever and is wearing a particularly striking pearl necklace. He comments on this with approval.

'Thank you,' she says. 'Isn't it gorgeous? I found it in a little antique jewellery shop near the office.'

'So she says,' puts in Simon, whose voice has thickened. Arnold sees he has brought the whisky to the table and the level has further descended.

'Simon,' Louise warns. 'Not here please.'

'Of course not.' Simon turns on her belligerently. 'Never *here*. Where do you suggest then? You're the one who's so good at arranging meetings, little trysts…' He refills his glass while everyone watches in startled silence.

'Simon,' says Louise, 'I do think you've had enough.'

'Yes I have,' he retorts. 'There's no doubt that I've had enough.'

'Simon!' Helena has emerged from the kitchen bearing the silver soup tureen. She glares at her son, uttering his name with such authority that he visibly quails and sets down his glass. 'Gosh, it's warm this evening,' she says, depositing the tureen on the sideboard and raising the lid to release an aroma that permeates the air like fragrant balm. The tension eases.

Arnold spoons the soup into his mouth and relishes the subtle blend of flavours. He wonders briefly about the reason for his son's uncharacteristic behaviour and considers instigating a man-to-man chat. On another occasion. The Scotch, meanwhile, has been discreetly removed to the sideboard and Simon is attending to his soup. The storm has subsided, and Helena ensures that it remains at bay. She introduces a benign conversation about traffic congestion and urban development, which leads to public transport and new technology. Microchips and mobile phones…

Then the doorbell peels. 'Ah!' Helena springs to her feet. 'That must be Evie.'

'Excellent,' says Arnold, tilting the bowl to extract the last of his soup. 'Now our party is complete.'

Evie looks unkempt, her father notices. Perhaps unkempt is too strong a word. Untidy. Untended. 'Sorry I'm late,' she says off-handedly. 'Where shall I sit?'

'Right here – next to me.' Arnold rises and pulls out her chair. 'Mademoiselle,' he says with a courtly bow.

She refuses his offer of soup and Helena, for a moment, looks perturbed. Only for a moment. 'Let's proceed to the next course,' she declares, regaining her composure. 'Arnold, will you check that the knives are sharp, dear? I'm going to ask you to carve the chickens.'

His stomach suddenly turns at the thought. He has carved lamb and beef and turkey, and would carve a buffalo if Helena deemed it necessary. His skill with the knife is masterly. But chicken? Who needs a man of his calibre to carve chicken? It's like inviting a brain surgeon to slice bread. But tonight isn't the night to argue, so Arnold obediently attends to the knives.

Then Helena appears with the trio of golden-brown birds arrayed on a vast silver platter, and Martin leads the appreciative chorus. Further acclaim greets the emergence of the roast potatoes and other accompanying dishes until, at last, the gastronomic line-up is complete. Arnold attends to the dissection of the fowl while Helena, assisted by Sandra, dispenses vegetables.

'Delicious,' proclaims Louise, who – being familiar with London's most fashionable restaurants – is the family's arbiter of taste. 'You must tell me how you do your seasoning, Helena. Chicken can sometimes be so bland.'

'Helena's a wonderful cook,' endorses Arnold. He is about to tuck into his serving when he notices that Evie's plate contains only vegetables. 'Helena,' he says, 'you haven't given our younger daughter chicken.'

'She didn't want any.'

'I don't eat meat any more,' Evie announces. 'I've become a vegetarian.'

'Ah.' Arnold glances round the table for the titters of amusement which he is sure will be forthcoming. 'A *vegetarian*?' Instead of mirth, though, his mocking repetition of the ridiculous label evokes silence. This infuriates him. 'All I can say, my girl, is that I have never heard of anything so silly in my life. If you had lived through the times I did, you wouldn't dream of such a thing. It's self-indulgence, that's what it is. Sheer self-indulgence.'

Evie shrugs, not bothering to respond, and rearranges the leaves on her plate. Arnold knows he should ignore her, but he cannot. It's as though he's being driven by an irresistible destructive force. 'The trouble with you is that your head's so full of causes and principles and big ideals that you've forgotten how normal people live.'

'Really?' She puts down her fork and regards him challengingly.

He notices that her face is devoid of make-up and her hair is lank and greasy. It enrages him. She enrages him. What a waste. 'Yes, really. If you paid some attention to your appearance and tried to be more pleasant to people, maybe you'd have found a husband by now.'

There's a shocked silence. Arnold's words seem to hang in the air. '*...a husband by now...*' He didn't mean to say that – not so brutally.

'I'm not looking for a husband.'

Evie is glaring at him, and is about to say more when Helena intercedes. 'Evie – Evelyn,' she says, 'let's not pursue this here. Arnold, I don't know what's got into you. Where's your tact?'

'I prefer him tactless,' says Evie in a cold, steady voice. 'For the first time in God-knows-how-long he has actually said what he means. Congratulations, father.'

Father? Since when does she call him father in that clipped and icy way? He bows his head and shakes it sadly.

'Look at me,' she demands. 'You started something. You were being honest with me, so I in return will be honest with you. Do you want to know why I'm not looking for a husband? Do you? Answer me!'

'Evie!' Helena breaks in, using exactly the same tone with which she earlier silenced Simon. And for the second time this evening it does its work. Evie's mouth closes into a thin straight line, her eyes narrow – but she doesn't say another word.

And Arnold, ashamed of his outburst and disturbed by the intensity of both his onslaught and Evie's response, gazes morosely at his plate. He wonders how he will get through the rest of the meal. His appetite seems to have fled. The others meanwhile regain their good spirit in a remarkably short time. They've got my resilience, thinks Arnold, watching how quickly his family bounces back. Evie remains quiet and Arnold vaguely nauseous, but the general level of bonhomie rises to such a crescendo that Helena has to restore order. She taps sharply on the table.

'We must press on with the next course,' she says. 'It's getting rather late for the children.'

Desserts are Helena's particular strength. Tonight an immense Pavlova is paraded before the assembly, followed by several smaller confections and a lead-crystal bowl filled with tropical fruit. 'This calls for pudding wine,' says Arnold, whose nausea has been superseded by a strange light-headedness.

'Jolly good idea,' enthuses Simon.

'I think so too,' says Sandra, holding out her glass. Arnold fills it generously, but is surprised by the relish with which she downs it. Sandra doesn't normally drink at all.

'You're not meant to…' Martin says to her in a low warning voice that everyone hears. But she deliberately proceeds to drain the glass.

'Sandra?' Helena looks at her questioningly. 'You aren't?'

'No.' She sets down her glass and covers her face with her hands. 'No, mother – I'm not pregnant. Two's quite enough.' She sniffs violently and makes for the door. 'I'm sorry,' she splutters, 'I'll be back in a minute.'

'What's that about?' Helena asks Martin. 'She's always been such a happy, placid person.'

He shrugs. 'She hasn't been lately … not very happy, I mean. The tablets have been helping, but they told her – they warned her – not to drink.'

'Well, well,' says Simon, who has regained access to the remains of the bottle of Scotch. 'Aren't we all in great shape? An adulteress here, and a depressive there, and a…'

'Simon!' This time Helena's admonition is verging on the shrill. 'Simon will you please shut up.'

It works. For the third time it works. But somehow the party fails to recover its vigour. Even the most robust resilience has its breaking point, thinks Arnold, who finds himself unable to say another word. Sandra reappears from the bathroom, red-eyed but otherwise composed, and the evening concludes shortly afterwards. Arnold remains seated at the empty table long after everyone has left.

'Aren't you coming to bed?' asks Helena. Several hours have passed.

Arnold looks up and sees that the Sabbath candles have burnt out. He nods. 'Nothing terrible has happened,' she says, placing a hand on his shoulder. 'Families will be families. People can't always be perfect.'

He shakes his head hopelessly. Perfection is one thing – but *this*? Simon, of course, is blameless. He needs to be firmer with Louise, and Arnold intends to tell him so. It's vital for a man to be able to count on his wife. As for Sandra – Arnold could have told her long ago, had told her in fact, that Martin wasn't the man for her. Not half the man. If she's unhappy now, there's nothing to be done. At least she has a husband.

Which is more than her sister has. What did Evie mean by asking, 'Do you know why I'm not looking for a husband?' in that harsh disdainful voice. It's bad enough that she's a feminist – has she now become a man-hater as well? Surely not Evie, who loves him? Or is it that Evie is a ... prefers *women*? If it's a condition like that, God forbid, it must be something that runs in Helena's family. It's nothing to do with Arnold, nothing at all.

'There's no point in sitting here and making yourself miserable,' Helena is saying with brisk authority. 'Apart from anything else, it's freezing. You'll catch cold. Come, Arnold – come to bed.'

He accepts the hand she offers and allows her to guide him upstairs.

And as he walks he sees ghosts. With each footstep, spectral beings rise to haunt him. They are laughing, pulling at his sleeve, telling him he deserves any unhappiness his family causes him. He is bound for punishment, damnation...

'It's not my fault,' he protests.

'No?' they scoff.

'No,' he cries. 'She was to blame. It was entirely due to her.'

'She?' they ask mockingly. 'She? Do you mean Evie... or Sandra... or Louise? Or was it Helena? *Was* it Helena? Tell us, Arnold – who is the *she* you are blaming?'

'It's ... Rachel...' For the first time in more than forty years, his lips shape her name. 'It's all her fault... she trapped me... it's Rachel's fault... Rachel... Rachel...'

II.

When did it start? Was there a particular moment when she ceased being the shy, fragile girl who whispered and tiptoed round him, hovering perpetually on the brink of ill-health? Was there a point when it struck him that beneath the demure lashes, straining under the prim white blouse, nestling behind the folds of skirt...?

'Isn't Arnost growing into a fine looking young man,' said Yetta, admiring his hair.

A fine looking young man. He sat up as tall as he could and cast an oblique, triumphant look at Hershel who could never be described as handsome. Then he glanced at Rachel, saw how she blushed and averted her gaze, and noticed for the first time the rise and fall of her chest.

Was *that* the moment?

Or was it later, perhaps three weeks later, when he was listening with some envy to a group of his school-fellows boasting about their female conquests? Arnost smiled superciliously, as though he had long graduated from such amateurish fumbling. 'One day,' he said, 'I'll tell you about the things *I* get up to with my landlady's daughter.' It was said without forethought – out of a need to have something to brag about more than any real intention to get up to anything with Rachel. Yet somehow, having made that announcement, Arnost couldn't stop thinking about the possibility. He noticed her eyes, the way her waistline curved, the shape of her breasts...

But that was normal, he told himself afterwards. A normal response by a healthy adolescent living in close quarters with an attractive, flirtatious young girl. He dreamed about her – nothing more than that, at first. Fantasies, nothing more, despite his idle boasts to the boys.

And it would have remained that way if Yetta hadn't got it into her head that Rachel needed to take regular walks. She needed fresh air and exercise for the pallor in her cheeks. And an escort, of course – for how could one contemplate sending a vulnerable female out walking on her own? Arnost was appointed to this role.

Thus it began. Week after week he walked chastely alongside her around the square, and tried to ignore the sensations aroused by her proximity. For distraction, he talked non-stop – almost entirely about himself. About the things he was learning at school and his plans for the future. He could see how much she admired his knowledge, and offered to take her to the museum for a chance to impress her further. Their walks grew longer, extending to the woodlands north of the town and even as far as the baths.

The first time he took her hand, he made it seem like an accident. Then he dared to kiss her on the cheek – just a small brotherly kiss. Then a more lingering embrace and more lingering still…

She didn't object. She never resisted an advance and he found that he was slightly disappointed by the ease with which she submitted. Also – despite being flattered – he became uneasy with the growing intensity of her responses and her frequent allusions to the depth of her feeling about him.

The final capitulation, though, was a triumph. A conquest worth all the tedious Saturday strolls, the clumsy and frustrating fiddling with her underclothes. At last. 'Rachel,' he panted, clinging to her, driving himself deep inside her and wanting her even more now that he had her. Feeling her wanting him. The two of them in the long grass, far away from anyone. 'Rachel, Rachel…'

'She's looking much better these days,' Yetta remarked with satisfaction. 'Don't you think so, Hershel? More robust, a better colour in her cheeks.'

'It must be all that fresh air she's getting with Arnost.'

Was there a hint of sarcasm in Hershel's response? What did he mean by that glance in Arnost's direction? Was it suspicion? Had Rachel told him?

She denied it when Arnost questioned her later. 'The thing about Hershel, though,' she pointed out, 'is that he *sees* things.'

'But we've been so careful.'

'Not actually seeing – it's more complicated than that. He has always been able to tell how I'm feeling – we've never had to talk about it. I think he's guessed about us – you and me. He mentioned to me the other day that there was someone, a student at the yeshiva, he thought would make a suitable husband for me.'

'And?'

'What do you mean *and*? I told Hershel that I'd only marry someone I loved. That was when he saw.'

And that was when Arnost saw it had gone too far. He decided to extricate himself from Rachel's affection. Marriage? Love? What was she thinking about? Arnost was going to university – he was destined for important things. Did she really imagine he would marry such a small-time small-town girl?

He tried to break the news gently. He said he adored her, but they had to be sensible, he had to be sensible. He needed to gain qualifications to make his way in the world. 'Don't cry, Rachel,' he said, trying to keep his voice soft and tender. 'It will be for the best.' He felt her tears dampening his shoulder and restrained an urge to push her away. She had no right to cling to him. It wasn't in the plan. 'Please don't cry,' he begged her.

But instead of abating, her tears became violent sobs. He held back his anger and tried to approach the situation as a test of his tolerance. She would exhaust herself soon and recover her composure. As a sensible person, surely she would see his point of view?

'Rachel…' he tried again, after a while.

She gasped something in response.

'Rachel, calm down – please calm down.'

She shut her eyes and drew a deep, shuddering breath. 'I'm pregnant, Arnost,' she managed at last. 'I'm carrying our child.'

He was cornered. Trapped. At first he disputed the fact of the pregnancy, then he denied responsibility.

'It's happened, Arnost,' she said, now completely calm. 'We must manage.'

Weren't there measures that could be taken – someone who could be paid to reverse what happened? He could ask his friends... ask around town... borrow money, if necessary...

'No.' She spoke with an authority that stunned him. Was this the same frail Rachel who had submitted to his every whim? What had happened to her? Had *he* done this to her? She was looking at him levelly and her tears had dried.

'Let's not make any decisions now,' he said uneasily, wishing she – the whole thing – would go away. Still in a state of disbelief. 'Are you *quite* sure?'

'Quite sure.'

'Have you told anyone else... your mother?'

'No, not yet. She saw that I was sick the other morning and believed me when I said I had a stomach upset. But she won't believe me for long.'

'And Hershel? You said he *sees* everything.'

'I don't know. He hasn't said anything – yet.'

They walked home in silence. Arnost remembered the way he had swaggered and strutted and boasted to her of his knowledge and achievements. He remembered the triumph of his conquest, his satisfaction at netting her, the gratification of boasting truthfully about his exploits with Rachel to the boys. And all the while she'd been laying her snare.

It had been agreed that she would break the news to her mother while Arnost waited in the adjoining room. He heard the murmur of their voices and it seemed hours before he was summoned.

Yetta's face was stern. 'And so? What do you have to say for yourself?'

Say? That was easy. As ever, even in the direst circumstances, words flowed effortlessly through Arnost's mouth. He loved Rachel, had always loved her, had been carried away by his passion, had hoped to marry her from the start, and would marry her now. Was there anything else he could do – under the circumstances?

'Nothing,' she said sadly, then immediately became businesslike. The wedding would have to take place very soon – as soon as Arnost completed his school-leaving examinations, which were imminent.

'And then?' he asked, for it seemed that the course of his punctiliously planned existence was now out of his control. It was being dictated to him by Rachel – by Yetta – by outside forces. In a single afternoon, self-directing Arnost had become a casualty of fate.

'And then?' repeated Yetta ironically. 'And then you'll be a husband and very soon, God willing, a father.'

A husband? A father? He was barely eighteen. He wanted to protest – to tell her that he couldn't do this, wouldn't. What right did she have to tell him what he should become? She wasn't his mother...

Instead he promised to do his best, and later repeated his pledge to Hershel.

'Do you mean it?' Hershel asked, holding Arnost's gaze. *Seeing* him.

'Of course I mean it.' Arnost squirmed angrily, resenting the interrogation. Surely it was enough that he had made the commitment and was doing the honourable thing?

'You won't let her down.' This was a statement rather than a question. A command.

'Why do you keep saying that? Don't you believe me?'

Hershel didn't answer. His scrutiny remained intense and unwavering. And Arnost was suddenly full of fear, desperate to escape – but, as in a nightmare, immobilised by Hershel's all-seeing blue eyes.

Which now – decades later – are fixed on him again. As he lies in the dark, they taunt him, making nothing of his wealth and success and his wonderful family. They threaten him. Soon the world will know what he did – what sort of man he really is.

'No,' he moans. 'Please... please.'

'Arnold, you're talking in your sleep.'

'Please leave me alone... let me be... please.'

'Wake up – you're having a bad dream.'

A dream? Are those blue eyes a dream? Is the darkness a dream? Is the dream darkness? If so, deliverance has come. He is being rescued. She has forgiven him and is pulling him back to the bright lights of the shore. 'Rachel,' he murmurs, turning towards her and burrowing his face in the softness of her breasts and the safety of her smell. 'It was so dark…'

'Hush,' Helena whispers, enveloping him and holding him tightly, enfolding him in a cocoon of such sweet solace that for the first time in ages he is urgently aroused. He returns her embrace with a passion that he feared was lost, thinking defiantly: I'm still strong, still in control, still able to outpace the night…

But the power proves fleeting, his potency a mirage. 'I'm sorry,' he mutters, having awoken, aroused and disappointed her. It is not an apology to *her*, though. He is aware of it even as he mouths the word. It is sorrow for himself. Grief. Loss. A lamentation almost too painful to bear.

'Don't worry about it,' says Helena, who quickly dismisses the incident and rearranges herself for sleep. 'It's not important.'

Worry about it? Worry about *it*? His failing strength, his failure to perform? Worry, anxiety, dread… 'Did you enjoy it anyway?' he asks, he has to ask. There must be some kind of counter to this galloping despair.

'It was fine,' she says, but he suspects she is lying.

'Good,' he says. 'I'm glad. I'm probably a little tense.'

'Forget about it now. It really doesn't matter.' She kisses him on the cheek, a gesture of finality. 'Sleep tight.' She resettles herself for the night.

But Arnold cannot sleep. I need a doctor, he thinks, cogitating in the dark. Should he consult a doctor? Is sexual failure a symptom or a cause? Or retribution? Is he finally being punished? Hershel's appearance, then that awful family dinner – and now this.

Ridiculous. Contemptuously, he dismisses such primitive superstition. Next thing he'll be worrying about the Scales of Justice and whether his name has been entered in this year's Book of Life. *Next* thing he'll be offering up a prayer.

The idea makes him smirk. And as he does so he becomes aware of the prickling sensation at the base of his neck that usually signals the onslaught of a psoriasis flare. He sits up sharply, for the prospect dismays him. He rummages in his bedside drawer for his medication.

'What *now*?' complains Helena, again disturbed from sleep.

'Nothing... I was sure I left some here... I can see that I'm going to be up all night.'

'What are you fussing about?'

'Sorry,' he mumbles. 'My pills – antihistamines – I seem to have run out.'

She groans and ducks beneath the bedclothes, which annoys Arnold. It's quite unlike her to ignore his distress. He fumes and fumbles with rising volubility until, with an incensed click, she turns on the light. 'Arnold, it's not necessary...' she begins.

'*Necessary*?' he interrupts. 'Have you any idea of the discomfort my condition can cause? Do you know what it's like to be kept awake all night, itching?'

'Calm down,' she says, 'you'll only make it worse.'

'You said you'd make an appointment for me to see Malcolm.'

'I will – tomorrow. Unless it's an emergency.'

'No,' he says abruptly – for he detects sarcasm and resents it. 'It's not an emergency.'

'Well then – lie back and relax and I'm sure you'll get to sleep.'

12.

While Arnold is fretting, Hershel is dreaming of the World to Come. The Almighty has welcomed him to his heavenly banquet and has set before Hershel the highest gastronomic reward for a virtuous life. It is a steaming dish of God's favourite sea monster, Leviathan. 'Eat and enjoy,' the Lord is saying. 'Leviathan has been my plaything, my pastime, my most wondrous creature of the deep. Now I'm serving its flesh to you the pious, as an afterlife treat.'

'Thank you Almighty,' Hershel says politely, and draws a small morsel towards his lips. But the smell is overpowering. How is a person, even a pious person, expected to swallow something that reeks so repulsively? Is God aware that His *pièce de resistance* smells so foul?

Apparently not, for He is gazing upon Hershel with eager delight, clearly anticipating his appreciation.

'It looks delicious,' he obliges.

'Good,' says the Lord. 'And how does it taste?'

Hershel tries to force a piece into his mouth. How can one sit in God's presence and refuse His Leviathan? On the other hand, wouldn't it be worse to eat and be sick? His stomach convulses at the thought. If he is exposed to this stench a second longer, he'll gag. Oh, the disgrace, the disappointment!

He awakes nauseous and perspiring. The putrid smell still hangs in the air, pressing on his chest and constricting his heart. Such a huge load of sorrow, such immense regret, such an enormous struggle to open his eyes!

He reaches full consciousness. It strikes him that the smell, which remains as potent as ever, has its source not in heavenly cuisine, but here, now. There is something rotten in his flat. Groaning, he pulls himself to his feet and, in the grey light of dawn, pads unerringly to the origin of the odour. 'Again,' he says aloud, vexed beyond measure. 'Not *again*.'

The door of his refrigerator is open, only slightly open but enough to admit an overpowering stench of decay into the flat. In the lukewarm recesses of the food compartment is an array of small dishes containing the uncovered remains of several solitary meals. A putrescent trio of sardines. A mouldy heap of herring in sour cream. A plate of decomposing salad. Holding his nose, Hershel hastily transfers the offending items to the bin. But when he dares to breathe again the smell is as potent as ever.

'Is this my life?' he demands in despair – his gaze directed challengingly aloft to a point far beyond the cracked ceiling. 'Is this what You planned for me – this squalor and misery? Never mind a decent refrigerator – can't You at least allow a man an enjoyable dream?'

Making an incensed noise, he deposits the contents of his bin to the larger one outside. A cat squalls. Hershel curses. It isn't the rotten food he minds so much – or the unreliable refrigerator. It's the dream. It has left him with an ache of disappointment that is far worse than the most disgusting smell. Even when he has finally sanitised the kitchen and kicked the refrigerator back to life, the ache lingers. Is it hunger, maybe? He doesn't *feel* hungry, but there's his strength to think about. A person can get weak.

'Why don't I set you up with Meals on Wheels?' that busybody Lily suggested in her charity voice. He dismissed the idea and insisted he was happy the way he was. He ate – he said – like a king. Such a king. She should see the delicacies now festering in his bin. He imagines Lily struggling between revulsion and solicitude, inadequately masking her disgust with concern. Which brings back to mind his own disguised aversion to God's paradisial offering, and this makes him aware of the ache again. That terrible ache…

It's disappointment, he decides as he settles down to serious contemplation and finally traces its origin. It's like the letdown a child experiences when a long-awaited gift proves to be a dud. The kingdom of heaven, bliss, paradise, all that anticipation – and *then* what? Even if Leviathan turns out to be the most delicious food, though, will that be enough?

Hershel thinks of the story of Bontshe Shvayg, whose life was such unmitigated misery that, in comparison, Hershel's seems idyllic. Bontshe suffered in silence. Poverty – disease – the death of loved ones: not once did he raise his voice in complaint. Which meant he was in line for a big reward when he finally reached heaven. His earthly track record was so remarkably clean that, after the trial of his soul in the Ultimate Court, Bontshe was invited to claim anything, anything at all, from the infinite array of heavenly prizes.

And what did he choose? Hershel smiles to himself at the recollection. All Bontshe wanted was to be served a hot buttered roll every morning of eternity. And what was the heavenly response to his choice? Hershel's smile disappears and he almost weeps for poor Bontshe. Instead of respectfully granting him his wish (So what if it was modest? So what if he wasn't greedy?), the Prosecuting Angels laughed him out of court.

Had Hershel been there he would have supported Bontshe Shvayg against the jeering cherubim or seraphim or whoever else saw fit to mock his humility. 'What do you want from a person? We're told that greed is bad, and now you're suggesting that virtue, too, is contemptible. So tell me – what are you suggesting Bontshe should have picked? A private jet? A house in the Caribbean? His own symphony orchestra?' In Hershel's humble opinion, the guarantee of one fresh buttered roll each day is nothing to be sneered at. And if the moral of the story is that a person shouldn't wait until after death to demand his due – well then, maybe Hershel should think again about Meals on Wheels. Maybe one shouldn't be proud.

The post arrives, which distracts him from further meditation. There's a catalogue advertising Greenstein's Passover Fare and a Final Demand from the Television Licencing Authority (despite the fact that Hershel has never owned or even rented a set). He's about to give vent to righteous indignation when another letter catches his eye. A pale lilac envelope with his name and address printed neatly by hand. Trying to guess its origins – and almost completely forgetting about his ache in the process – he opens it and extracts a single sheet. Perfumed. He sniffs it. Then he reads it, and his indignation grows with every line:

> Dear Hershel,
>
> I know you won't mind my addressing you informally. After our chat last week I feel certain we are now on friendly terms at the very least. I so much enjoyed meeting you and, as I said several times, I am determined to help you in whatever way I can.
>
> I'm sure you'll be pleased to know that the response to my Presentation at the Board Meeting last Thursday was extremely positive. There was a great outpouring of sympathy for your plight and a decision was taken to write to the synagogue on your behalf. So let's pray.
>
> The main reason I'm writing now, though, is not about your future but about your past.
>
> You see, Hershel, I have been appointed Launch Co-ordinator for

our exciting new Heritage Centre and am absolutely brimming with ideas for the opening events. One of the concepts that kept popping up during a recent brainstorming session with my Sub-Committee was (not surprisingly) the days of yore. And each time the concept came up I thought of you.

To me, Hershel, you are our days of yore. After we met I had a strong sense of coming into contact with a genuine piece of history. Truly. Anyway, I talked things over with Helena Rose (our Chair), Betty Wilson (our Hon Sec) and Bernard Kaplan (the new Cantor who is also a technology expert) and it was unanimously agreed that I should invite you to join our Sub-Committee in an advisory capacity.

So this is my formal invitation which I very much hope you will accept. It will be wonderful for us to have someone like you to be our (so to speak) sounding-board. And it will be extremely beneficial for you to have a new interest in your life. As we charity workers frequently remind one another: one gets out of something as much as one is prepared to put into it!

Congratulations and welcome to our ranks! I shall be in touch very soon with details of our first planning meeting.

Yours, Lily Sanderson.

Hershel slams the letter down angrily. 'Is she *crazy*?' he demands aloud. Is this what Hershel Fine has struggled through life for – to become, never mind a relic or a piece of history, but a sounding-board? A *so-to-speak* sounding-board? And what sounds do these noble philanthropists think Hershel will make about those days of yore he is meant to represent? Harmonious sounds? Comforting sounds? Sentimental sounds like he's on stage in *Fiddler on the Roof*? 'Isn't it sad,' they'll say, wiping away tears, 'how it's all gone – lost – extinguished, such a quaint way of life.'

Isn't it wonderful of these generous benefactors to be doing so much to preserve at least the memories? Surely it's incumbent on Hershel to make everything as cosy and palatable as he can?

Well, he won't. He refuses. Someone else can supply them with the things they want to hear. Hershel's *days of yore* is not the stuff of musical comedy. Tales of *his* past will certainly not evoke nostalgic tears. Poverty isn't romantic. Nor is persecution, fear, betrayal and death.

Anyway, why suddenly are they so interested? What has caused this outpouring of affection for *once-upon-a-time*? As far back as Hershel can remember since arriving in this country, he has always perceived himself to be an embarrassing sort of Jew, lacking refinement, secular intellect, ambition – not to mention acceptable elocution. Why on earth do they now want him to take the fun out of their Heritage Centre with truth?

Dear Mrs Sanderson,

I am sorry to refuse your invitation for me to join your committee. I cannot see myself as your guide to a golden yesteryear, because for me the 'days of yore' weren't exactly golden.

A suggestion though: Maybe it will be helpful for you to get hold of the plans for the Jewish Museum that was established in Prague by the Germans. It was intended to be a memorial to an extinct race. They were a very efficient people, the Germans, I can assure you.

As for the other matter (my future), I want you to understand that it is not worth troubling yourself about it any further. Let me explain: every day, three times a day, sometimes more, a Jew prays for the return to Jerusalem. In addition to that, all the time he prays for the coming of the Messiah. This kind of longing has sustained our people. 'The main thing is yearning,' one of our great rabbis once said.

So, Mrs Sanderson, if that is the situation, does it make any difference where Hershel Fine does his yearning? A mansion, a flat, an old-age home? What is – or was – is nothing compared with what will be.

Sincerely, Hershel Fine.

He signs his name with a flourish and, for a moment, feels better. Wouldn't he love to see her face when she reads it and reports back to her diligent Hon Sec and her glamorous Chair…

The thought transports Hershel back to the hotel gathering and the speech by Madame Chair. Such poise. Such panache. And Lily asking him whether he knows her, and he replying that he knows the type. The type? Confident. Successful. Would Arnost Rosenbaum have settled for any other type? Yet there was Rachel – as unlike Helena Rose as it is possible for two women to be…

Hershel believed he knew Rachel. He thought he knew her through and through. Yet while he was dreaming with his head in the clouds, trying to be like Jacob who climbed to heaven and wrestled with angels – back on earth, under his very nose…

13.

It wasn't a shock, for Hershel doubts whether he's ever had the capacity to be shocked. It was bafflement by the fact that it had been going on for so long and was so far advanced, without his awareness. Surely someone who prided himself on his ability to *see* things should have anticipated this?

Not that he was ignorant about such matters. Desire and betrayal and unlawful consummation are common currency in the Old Testament and the Talmud. Even then, Hershel understood perfectly why Sarah eavesdropped and Miriam told tales and Rachel envied Leah and Dinah enticed the Hivite. He gave discourses on the subject.

But when it came to his sister, his small pale sister…

Surely not? Not Arnost and her? It wasn't possible.

'Rachel has something to tell you,' said his mother.

Hershel studied Yetta with trepidation, for her voice sounded ominous. Rachel, however, spoke with total composure: 'We're getting married – Arnost and me.'

'Married?' Hershel almost choked on the word. What was she talking about – *married*? Hadn't he told her he'd made preliminary arrangements for his friend Avram to meet her with a view to matrimony? And to Arnost? Why *Arnost*? Why on earth would she want such a nobody for a husband, such a young penniless stray? 'I don't understand.'

'I love him, Hershel.'

'You love him?'

She nodded and he saw her resolve, her seriousness. And he believed her, feeling sadness that Arnost should be the recipient of such love.

'I'm pregnant, Hershel,' she added so softly that he had to ask her to repeat the words. Then he exploded. So *this* was the reason for her great and undying love, such a hasty marriage? What had that idiot done to her? How did he dare... after all the kindness and charity they'd shown towards him, the sacrifices they had made to give him a home?

'I loved him from the start,' Rachel said quietly. 'I loved him before this happened. It's not just – because...'

'Don't talk to people about the pregnancy, Hershel,' Yetta put in quickly. 'It's early. We can arrange the wedding soon. No one needs to know.'

He shook his head, stunned and helpless. He should have known – suspected. He'd had an inkling there was something going on with all the walks together and Rachel looking so happy, so buoyant all of a sudden. He'd even joked about it (such a joke) without imagining...

What a fool. Because Hershel was inexperienced in these matters, did it mean his sister would remain innocent too? She *seemed* so innocent, though – *behaved* so innocently. If Hershel wasn't aware that despite her frail physique, Rachel had great strength of character, he would assume she had been led astray.

Rage burnt through him as he recalled Yetta's admiration of the boy, her trust in him, the comfort and affection Hershel himself had offered the sad cuckoo in their nest. Who had grabbed everything – their food, their shelter, their affection, and now his sister. Couldn't he have practised on someone else – somewhere else – preferably very far away? He didn't deserve Rachel's love.

He positioned himself squarely in front of Arnost and looked directly into his eyes. 'You say you'll do your best?'

Arnost nodded, fidgeting uncomfortably.

'Do you mean it?'

What did Hershel expect – that the boy would say *no*? Of course he didn't. He insisted that he would take care of Rachel to the best of his ability, forever. And Hershel, because there was no point doing otherwise, tried to believe him and pretended to be happy. After all it was a wedding, and Rachel seemed happy and even Yetta seemed happy...

'Hershel, cheer up,' Yetta urged as the preparations proceeded and an air of excitement pervaded the home. She sat down to catch her breath; Hershel noticed how frequently Yetta sat down to catch her breath.

'With such a miserable face,' she gasped, 'a person would think we were planning a funeral.'

Weddings, funerals, comings, goings, people passing through. The punctuation marks of life, thinks Hershel. How many such rites of passage has he watched from his caretaker's flat? Joy, tragedy, secrets...

All irrelevant, insignificant, when – with a flick of her wrist – Destiny can obliterate them and alter forever the course of existence.

Blessed art thou, O Lord, who sanctifies thy people by the rite of the canopy and the sacred covenant of wedlock.

Does the Lord look down each time? Does He peer through each flower-bedecked canopy, smiling on love, scowling at hypocrisy, planning punishment for subterfuge? Did He, for instance, watch the wedding of Arnost and Rachel on a cold Sunday in 1937 and know their fate? Did He shape their future? Did He gaze deep into Arnost's heart or deep into Rachel's womb – or was He distracted by the shouting of Hitler and the fate of all the babes in wombs who would never see their own wedding day?

Soon O Lord our God may there be heard in the cities of Judah and in the streets of Jerusalem the voice of joy and gladness, the voice of the bridegroom and the voice of the bride, the jubilant voice of bridegrooms from their canopies and of youths from their feasts of song.

There was little rejoicing in the streets of Nyíregháza. It was a private wedding, hastily assembled and modest in scale. Hershel remembers neither the prayers nor the festivities. He will never forget, though, the sound of glass shattering beneath the bridegroom's heel as the climax to the ceremony. The glass was crushed to symbolise the destruction of the ancient Temple in Jerusalem, but to Hershel it was a portent of what lay ahead...

Blessed art thou, O Lord, who makest the bridegroom to rejoice with the bride.

...Or maybe that's hindsight. How easy, in retrospect, to imbue the splintering of glass with significance. Awaiting them – all of them, not just the bridal couple – was not a heel but an axe that was to smash down upon the length of their days. And the shards – millions of tiny shards – would scatter everywhere.

But who knew it then? Who predicted it? Even in Germany where the Nazis were crying 'Death to the Jews!', they didn't believe it. Not yet. In Poland they were casting wary eyes to the border, where tanks were amassing. Hitler's army was limbering up for a fray. And Hungary, still nursing a twenty-five year old grudge about the loss of land following the Treaty of Trianon, was looking to strutting Admiral Horthy to heal bruised national pride. Hungary for the Hungarians, he bellowed – whispering, meanwhile, to Germany and Italy that the restoration of his country's might could be mutually beneficial.

The issue of a Greater Hungary did not much concern the inhabitants of Yetta's house in Nyíregháza. There were more immediate matters. The build-up to the wedding had been engrossing, exciting – there was happiness, in a pent-up sort of way. But then came afterwards...

Hershel recalls the silence that followed the departure of the last guest, the way they sat – Rachel, Arnost, he and Yetta – without saying a word, not knowing what to say. Rachel looked exhausted but kept glancing lovingly at her new husband, touching his arm, his face. Arnost's gaze was mostly averted. He fidgeted uneasily and then, from time to time (as though remembering his new status), gave Rachel a reassuring smile. Yetta sat slumped, her eyes intermittently shutting, struggling against the breathlessness that seemed to be worsening each day.

And Hershel? What did *he* feel or say or do on that auspicious day? Nothing particular – other than experience an acute awareness of the futility of railing against what had happened or what might come. What will be, will be, he conceded. But he prayed harder than ever before for God to see fit to guard them – *all* of them – from harm.

Not that God heard him. Who could blame Him, though, for being distracted that day? He had troubles far greater than the concerns of a family in Nyíregháza. Yetta's health, Rachel's baby, Arnost's fidelity and Hershel's future as a scholar were tiny matters compared with the colossal tide of suffering that God was battling to hold back.

He fought and He failed. It was a triumph for suffering, a defeat for God. Or maybe He didn't try very hard, maybe He sat back and allowed the tide to do its work just as He did in the time of Noah. The same bellowing, vengeful Yahweh, who kept His people dutiful with a rod of iron. Fair-minded Yahweh who saved pious Noah from the flood. Would a fair-minded Yahweh have bothered to save Arnost Rosenbaum from the flames?

Hershel sighs. It doesn't make sense and never will. On the other hand, sense isn't necessarily the same as truth. And truth... His head hurts. Truth, it is said, is everywhere – all over the world. Why? Because like the wandering Jew it was expelled from one place after another and is forced to roam – and roam.

If only it would continue on its way and stop bothering Hershel Fine. Hasn't he had enough in his life? He'll never be without sadness, for it has permeated his bones and will never leave him. But he'd have thought by now that his anger would have dissipated. Surely, after all the years...?

Irritably, Hershel pulls himself to his feet. He decides once and for all to halt the train of recollection that the encounter with Arnold has provoked. It's unpleasant, unhealthy and pointless. There are more important matters to address. He needs to check that the synagogue is prepared for the Sabbath services. He has his reputation to think about. For fifty years, he has been an exemplary caretaker and he won't let Arnost or Arnold or whatever he wants to call himself distract him from his duties now.

Hershel leaves his flat and, holding his hat against the gusting wind, makes his way along the open passageway towards the synagogue. A chubby stranger suddenly emerges from the shadows, blocking his path.

'Ah – here you are, Mr Fine. They told me I'd find you somewhere around. I want to introduce myself.'

He extends a plump damp hand. Hershel takes it reluctantly.

'I'm Bernard Kaplan, the new Cantor.'

'Ah.' Hershel nods, remembering. 'The technology expert.'

Bernard laughs modestly. 'The word has spread then – I suppose one could say it's a field that holds my interest, but I'm hardly an expert.' He pauses in anticipation of Hershel's insistence on his technological aptitude, but this is not forthcoming.

'You want I should show you around?' he asks instead.

'No, no – not exactly. I've been in the synagogue several times – as an applicant for my job, as a congregant and as a member of the Museum Committee, which – er – um...' He breaks off in some confusion, recalling Hershel's association with – or dissociation from – the Museum. 'Anyway,' he continues after an uncomfortable pause, 'the reason for my presence is to do some of the groundwork, so to speak, for a survey I've been asked to undertake.'

'I see,' says Hershel, who doesn't at all and wishes the man would say what he wants without all this bush-beating. Does he think Hershel has nothing better to do?

'It's a technological survey,' Bernard explains. 'There's been a fair bit of excitement about some of my ideas for installing various devices in different areas of the museum. Some voice-activated, others with touch pads...'

'Listen, Mr... Cantor – Friday morning is not good for me, as you can imagine. Can I help you or can I not help you?'

'I need access to the synagogue, please. For about half-an-hour at the most. Before I can proceed with anything else I need to check the energy sources.'

Hershel smiles, for the irony amuses him. Bernard beams back, assuming approval. 'So,' he says eagerly, 'can I begin?'

'Come with me.' Hershel extracts the keys from his pocket.

'Thank you very much,' says Bernard, trotting breathlessly alongside him with a briefcase in one hand and a folded newspaper in another. 'I'll be as quick as I possibly can. Would you like to have a look at this while you're waiting? It's today's *Jewish Chronicle* – I collected it on my way.'

Minutes pass. Hershel, leaning against the synagogue door, leafs idly though the newspaper. Another power struggle in the upper reaches of the Board of Deputies. More violence in the Middle East. He yawns, wishing mister Cantor would finish with his inspection. Enough's enough already. There's work to be done.

Suddenly he stops short. Something has caught his eye. A photograph. A man and a woman smiling side by side and, beneath the picture, several paragraphs of text:

LEADING COMPANY DIRECTOR RETIRES
AFTER FORTY-FIVE YEARS.

Widespread acclaim has been lavished on 77-year-old Hungarian-born Arnold Rose (pictured above with his wife Helena) who recently stepped down after more than 45 years at the helm of one of the country's most successful textile companies.

When Mr Rose's association with Fabrico Limited began, it was a small family business owned and managed by Mr Walter Rothman and his brother Ivan. Since then it has grown into a multinational company specialising in household linens and furnishing fabrics. Arnold Rose, according to one of his closest colleagues, was largely responsible for this expansion.

'He had the vision and foresight to see the possibilities for growth and the energy to make it happen,' said Mr Jonathan Fielding, who has taken over as managing director of the company.

Arnold Rose was born and grew up in a small town in northeast Hungary. His further education was cut short by the Second World War, which he survived mostly in hiding in Budapest.

He moved to England after the War, joining the small staff of Fabrico Limited in 1948. Three years later, after the sudden death of Mr Walter Rothman, he was appointed to the Board.

Mr Rose married Helena, only daughter of Mr Ivan Rothman, in 1954. The couple has three children, all living in London. Mrs Rose is a prominent member of the Jewish Women's Management Guild and various other service organisations. She is currently heading the fund-raising committee for the new Jewish Heritage Centre to be officially opened in the East End of London next year.

14.

Very nice, thinks Hershel, leaning against the door-post. Weak, almost collapsing he's so weak. A very nice story. Poor boy starts with nothing, marries boss's daughter and takes over boss's company. He turns it from a small family business into a mega-operation and then graciously retires. Three children in London. Wonderful – excellent – well done.

Nice, simple, smooth. Who would want to sully such a heart-warming story with the spectres of reality? Didn't someone once say that a beautiful lie is sometimes preferable to the debasing truth? Someone clever, but not nearly as clever – as unbearably clever – as Arnold Rose.

The newspaper slides from Hershel's hand to the floor, and he feels himself slipping from consciousness.

'Very nice,' comments Helena, glancing at the article over a later-than-usual breakfast. 'The photograph, I must say, is not entirely flattering. But the write-up is really rather nice.'

Arnold, across the table, is dismembering a kipper. It is one of his particular pleasures, dismembering kippers. 'What?' he asks absently. 'What's nice?'

'This piece in the *Jewish Chronicle*. About you.'

'Me?' He sits up. 'What do they say about me? Let me see it.'

Helena laughs. 'Don't get so agitated. It's nothing to worry about. I told you – it's rather pleasing. Here – look.'

He takes hold of the newspaper, struggling to hide the anxiety that suddenly, ridiculously, rises. Yes, it *is* pleasing, he tells himself as he studies the photograph and skims the text. A picture of a contented couple, the potted biography of a successful man. A man with vision and foresight and energy... 'It's odd,' he remarks, 'to see one's life condensed into so few words.'

'It is, rather,' says Helena, who has turned her attention to *The Times*. At her level of communal prominence, an appearance in the *Jewish Chronicle* is not great cause for excitement. 'The girl – the reporter who phoned – kept me for ages with her questions. I tried to be patient, but I knew they'd only use a tiny bit. Oh, the time one wastes!'

Arnold decisively folds the paper and returns to his kipper. But the anxiety does not leave him. It worsens, spoiling the taste of his food and the serenity of his morning. Abruptly he picks up the newspaper again and begins to reread the piece.

'What's the matter?' asks Helena vaguely. 'They didn't get something wrong, did they? Honestly, these journalists...'

'No, no. Not at all. It's all accurate – perfectly correct.' Arnold's eyes travel slowly from word to word, from sentence to sentence. It *is* accurate, he thinks. Quite accurate. He *was* born and raised in a small Hungarian town and survived the War mostly in hiding... hiding what? He shudders.

'What *is* it, Arnold?' Helena asks, now slightly irritable. 'You *are* making a fuss about that silly article. I think your trouble is that you're underemployed these days. We're going to have to find things to occupy your mind.'

Arnold smiles. He forces himself to smile. 'Why don't you concern yourself with your own mind, dear?' he says with some acerbity. 'I'm quite content with the level of activity in mine.' He doesn't quite achieve his usual level of disdain. Even so, she seems reassured, for it is more normal for Arnold to be scathing than troubled. Sniffing haughtily, she returns to the arts pages of *The Times.*

'They say here that the new *Hamlet* at the National is quite outstanding,' she murmurs. 'I must try to get tickets.'

Bernard Kaplan, meanwhile, has come upon the comatose caretaker. 'Mr Fine – are you all right? Here – let me help you to a chair.'

Hershel feels someone gripping his arm. He sees the newspaper on the floor and remembers the picture, the text – the bland, hollow words. And behind them, echoing in his head, those unwritten: the wife and child excised from the authorised history of Arnold Rose.

'You gave me a terrible fright, you know.' Bernard peers closely at Hershel, looking extremely concerned.

'I'm sorry. I don't know what came over me.'

'It's lucky I found you when I did. By sheer coincidence, I was wanting to ask you about the electricity supply for the Eternal Flame – but never mind about that now. Has this happened before?'

Hershel shakes his head.

'I wonder what it could have been.' Bernard scratches his head. 'Perhaps you should wait here while I call for help.'

The prospect of being tended by an altruist is enough to propel Hershel back to his feet. 'I'm quite all right now,' he declares. 'I was feeling a little funny for a minute or two – the stuffiness maybe, it sometimes affects me. But now I'm perfectly fine.'

'Are you sure?' Bernard studies him doubtfully.

'Absolutely. As a matter of fact...' Hershel thinks hard, desperate to construe some means of dismissing this man and returning to his flat. 'As it happens, I've just remembered several things that I haven't yet done – it's Friday, as you know.'

As Bernard knows. What else can he do but offer to postpone his energy inspection till next Monday? And what else can Hershel do but volunteer to have his health professionally screened? As he waves Bernard off, he notices the newspaper still spread on the floor where he dropped it. He picks it up.

'I'm off,' announces Arnold, impatient to set the day in motion and thus relieve by displacement activity his persistent, nagging anxiety.

'Oh?' Helena sounds surprised. 'What's the rush? Have another kipper.'

'No, thank you. I must get going at once or else I shall be late.' He leaves the room, lying importantly about meetings and investment schemes and various people scheduled to see him.

Helena remains seated, sedately sipping tea. 'Arnold,' she calls, as he's about to open the front door.

'What is it? Quickly...'

'Would you be an angel and pick up my order from the fishmonger on your way home? We're having people for dinner tomorrow and I thought I'd do trout.'

He agrees reluctantly, for it has always seemed to him a sign of weakness for men to run errands for their wives. Then he steps outside and accelerates his pace until he is striding fast and breathing hard. Walking off his disgruntlement as well as that grumbling anxiety. Walking, walking, until – tentatively – he tries thinking again about the newspaper article that evoked such disturbing sensations and notes with immense relief that he is now able to remain composed. Excellent, he thinks, moving faster, not sure where he is heading or why. It hardly matters though, for his head has cleared and his optimism has returned. That's better. He has come through, using his tried and tested strategy: moving onward, ever onward, neither looking back or glancing from side to side. A man of foresight and energy…

'Oi! Fucking idiot! Can't you see where you're going? You'll get yourself fucking killed!'

A motorcyclist has skidded to a halt, narrowly missing him. Arnold gives him a withering look and continues on his way.

Hershel re-reads the article and this time, instead of weakening him, it provokes anger more intense than he has experienced for years. Far from wanting to hide from Arnold and the mixture of grief and pity and rage his reappearance has inspired, Hershel is now impelled to confront him, to challenge him with the truth. Does she know – this Helena, this accomplished and prominent Mrs Rose – that there was once a predecessor? Is she aware of the first Mrs Rose? Or, to be accurate, Mrs Rosenbaum – which is a Rose by another name.

Maybe he'll write to her. Dear Mrs Rose, he'll say. My dear Mrs Rose, Apologies for troubling you, such a busy woman, but there's something possibly you should know about the early life of your husband…

No. That won't do. It's sneaky, cowardly, will maybe punish the wife more than Arnost himself. Anyway, he'll deny it all – doesn't Hershel know him through and through? He'll deny it with absolute conviction – and who would believe a mad caretaker over an important company director?

Wearily, Hershel sits down to consider an alternative outlet for his anger, then notices on his table the letter to Lily Sanderson that he penned in such burning fury. Suddenly it occurs to him that he has the perfect means to confront Arnold. If he really wants to, that is.

Arnold, in the meantime, is pleasantly engaged in light conversation with the morning habitués of his Mayfair club. He listens with pride to his own adeptness at guiding and maintaining the pace and direction of the talk from the general to the particular and back to the general again. It's like a choral symphony, he thinks, seeing himself as the nimble-wristed conductor – so sensitive, so in tune. The topics, he is aware, are hardly of an elevated nature, being second-hand cogitation on current affairs. It's the style, though – the flavour, the detail, the flair. After all, artists don't restrict themselves to lofty themes. On the contrary…

'How's the wife?' someone asks.

The wife? For a moment Arnold is lost. Crazily, his mind goes blank. Then, like a jigsaw reassembling itself piece by piece, comes a mental reproduction of the photograph accompanying the retirement article. A man and his wife. The man visibly pleased with himself. *Vainglorious*, thinks Arnold, relieved to locate the perfect word. And she at his side, with that commanding look of hers, a chairman through and through.

'Wife not well, then?'

Arnold starts, for he has unintentionally winced. 'Oh, no,' he says quickly. 'You mean Helena? She's perfectly well, thank you.'

Hastily he retrieves the conversational baton, but the spell has been broken. Instead of seeing himself as an invincible *artiste* of the spoken word, he now surveys the scene from a vertiginous height. And in his head there is a mocking voice that jeers at his pomposity and ridicules his pretensions. 'I shall have to leave very soon,' he says at last, straining after an air of harried importance. 'I have an appointment back in Chelsea in less than an hour.'

As he puts on his coat, he wonders whether it is too early to collect Helena's order from the fishmonger. He wants to go home.

With some regret, Hershel discards his original letter to Lily and takes out a clean sheet of paper. *Dear Lily*, he writes with deliberate informality, having grudgingly decided that truth comes before pride. Anyway, his ironic allusion to German excesses and Jewish longing would be wasted on someone like her…

> With much regret I have to tell you that maybe you should ask somebody else to be your pet traditional Jew. You see, my memories of the days of yore, which you seem so keen to celebrate, are not as sweet as perhaps you would wish. There is someone else you could approach, though. As it happens, I was looking at the *Jewish Chronicle* today and what should I see but an article about someone who was quite close to me in those bygone days? Coincidentally, he is the husband of your chairman Helena. What a small world! Anyway, it occurs to me that if you want a better, more optimistic picture of the past you should invite this Arnold Rose to join your history team. And tell him if you see him that Hershel sends greetings and best wishes on his retirement. To his wife as well. Tell him also that I look forward to seeing him soon so that we can catch up on old times.
>
> Yours sincerely, Hershel Fine.

15.

'I cannot for the life of me understand why Lily Sanderson and her dreary husband have to be invited to every single dinner party we give,' grumbles Arnold, who has been assigned the task of shining cutlery. This is not something he generally agrees to, but somehow he is finding himself increasingly acquiescent to Helena's bidding. This new compliance troubles him during the rare moments he thinks about it. Mostly, though, he keeps his mind otherwise distracted and congratulates himself from time to time on how well he is handling his retirement.

The mention of Lily, however, has set his anxiety going again. Even the idea of her makes Arnold itch.

'Lily has never been anything but a perfect guest,' says Helena primly as she tweaks the floral centrepiece. 'She is lively, interested, sometimes moderately interesting – and tonight, especially, we need someone like her.'

'Tonight?' Arnold's itch worsens. 'Why tonight?'

'We have a potentially *lethal* combination – boring beyond compare. Various people connected with the museum and the synagogue – honestly, Arnold, I'm finding all this increasingly tedious. I'm rather sorry I took it on.'

'Really?' he asks, rather glad.

'The Red Cross has asked me to head one of their campaigns – which I think I'll do as soon as we've got this thing off the ground. Ah, well – Bernard's coming at any rate, and he's terribly sweet.'

'Terribly sweet,' echoes Arnold sardonically as, without thinking, he directs the fork he is polishing at a particularly raw spot inside his collar.

'Arnold!' Helena is shocked. 'What *are* you doing?'

He becomes conscious of the gesture and after an instant of embarrassment grows angry. 'Helena, I've told you for days – *weeks*, in fact – how bad my psoriasis is and how generally unwell I've been feeling. But you, with all your good works, can't find the time to make an appointment for me to see a doctor. A simple phone call – that's all I ask for.'

'I have,' she says quietly. 'I've spoken to Malcolm and he'll see you next Thursday.' She holds out her hand to retrieve the unsanitary fork, which she takes to the kitchen for ablution. 'I'd appreciate it, Arnold,' she calls over her shoulder, 'if you made an effort to be polite this evening.'

'Polite?' He follows her testily. 'Since when have I ever been other than polite? Oh – you mean in case you take it into your head to retire upstairs with your – your Game Boy?' He laughs, pleased with his witticism.

'Really, Arnold,' says Helena severely, 'Bernard is half my age and happily married. And so, I've always believed, am I. You're behaving most peculiarly these days. So many people have said nice things to me about you since that piece appeared in the *JC*. I can't imagine *what* they'd think if they could see the way you've been carrying on lately.'

'What are you talking about? What nice things?'

'Oh, I don't know. About how interesting it was to read about you instead of me for a change. And how fascinating it sounded, being in hiding in Budapest. And how exceptional it was for you to have done so well in a new country... Arnold, would you please hurry with that cutlery – I have a million glasses I need you to shine.'

He returns to his task, partly mollified by the praise. But uneasy still. Gripped by the unspecific apprehension which has taken root inside him like a restless and sporadically hungry parasite. 'I hope...' he begins, but cannot continue for what he hopes is elusive and indefinable.

'What?' asks Helena, who cannot resist chasing random thoughts.

'Nothing,' he says crossly – then considers for a moment. 'I very much hope my early life is not going to be the topic of tonight's conversation.'

'Oh, Arnold – you are funny.' She comes up behind him and ruffles his hair, then kisses him affectionately on the cheek. 'You're such a curious mixture of arrogance and modesty. The reason everyone's so interested is that they admire you so much. And – by the way...' she begins to giggle uncontrollably and has to sit down, for it seems she cannot stop.

'By the way – what?' asks Arnold in alarm, for her uncharacteristic hysteria is worrying.

'Lily,' she manages to say. 'Lily told me she's got a surprise for you. God knows what it could be – she refused point-blank to elaborate. I'm sure you can't wait.'

Arnold feels his itch starting up again. His anxiety and his itch are in discordant concert, tearing at his innards and tugging at his skin. 'God,' he says through clenched teeth, 'how I wish that woman would mind her own business. Can't she leave me alone?'

Helena stops laughing. 'I think you're taking all this much too seriously,' she says. 'I know you're not feeling entirely well, dear, but there's no need to lose your sense of humour. Lily is a very well meaning person, but she's hardly worth such a fuss. Can't you humour her – for my sake, please? Surely that's not asking too much?'

He doesn't answer. Instead he focuses his attention on the remaining items of cutlery. He makes sure that each cutting edge is gleaming and imagines how cleanly he would slice into Lily Sanderson's neck.

An hour later he learns that Lily unfortunately – *most* unfortunately –

will be unable to attend the dinner as she has somehow injured the very subject of his incisional fantasy. 'Lily,' announces Helena, 'has just telephoned to say that she has hurt her neck.'

For an instant Arnold is intrigued by the possibility that he has somehow wished this upon her – that he has this power, this potential. Then he catches himself. It's coincidence. A small joke played by fate.

He laughs euphorically. Isn't it good to have fate on one's side? The prospect of Lily's absence cheers him so much that he rubs the glasses till they sparkle. Then he decants the wine. Finally, he attends to his toilette with such relish that Helena, hearing him humming and splashing in the shower, calls out how glad she is to note his improvement in mood.

'Poor Lily,' everyone says when they hear about her affliction. Which elicits comment about her particular susceptibility to spinal maladies. It also inspires recollections from those who have been similarly struck, and leads to observations about other especially vulnerable parts of the body. The joints, the arteries, the kidneys, the heart...

'We're getting old, that's our trouble,' sighs Bertha Lawrence, who is diligently countering the grief of recent widowhood with a series of cruises to tropical parts. She has never looked better.

'Old? Who's old?' retorts Helena, offering greetings and giant stuffed olives and crudités and dips. Arnold is seeing to the drinks.

'Not you, Helena darling,' says Bertha. 'You're a spring chicken compared to me. And Arnold – Arnold, I couldn't believe it when I saw your age mentioned in that delightful piece in the – where was it? – was it *The Telegraph*?'

'The *Jewish Chronicle*.'

'That's right. Goodness – I've always assumed you were at least twenty years younger. How do the two of you manage to stay so youthful?'

Arnold shrugs offhandedly and plies her with another drink, resisting the urge to point out the vulgarity of discussing a person's age. He refuses to let Bertha Lawrence's tactlessness topple his hard-won equanimity. However boorish she is, it is nothing – absolutely nothing – compared with the steam-rollering crassness to which he would have been subjected if Lily were here. He can manage Bertha – and the Kings and Frank Singer. He can even manage the puppy-dog Cantor who persists (is the man a moron?) in gazing devotedly at Helena, hanging on to her every word. With Lily Sanderson out of the way the evening will be a cinch.

'So how are your lovely children?' someone asks during a companionable lull between the hors-d'oeuvre and the entrée. Since Helena is adjusting seasonings in the kitchen, Arnold is forced to take the question.

'Fine,' he says automatically, aware of stirrings of unease. 'Excellent. Very well indeed.' Until now he has always felt a satisfying glow at the mention of the children or any allusion to their achievements. Now he is disinclined to think or talk about them. He and Helena have not discussed them at all since that unpleasant Friday night supper. From time to time he has heard Helena conversing on the phone with Simon or his sisters, but it has been tacitly understood that Arnold is unavailable for consultation. He prefers it that way.

'How about that sweet little Evie?' Maxine Singer is saying. 'Goodness – I remember that child on the stage. I always wondered where she'd got that talent. Was it from your side of the family, Arnold? Are you the musical one?'

'Well – not exactly. I enjoy music, of course.'

'Arnold,' interrupts Helena, marching in with a laden tray, 'has taught me everything I know about music. He's the most cultured person I've ever met.'

'Helena, really,' protests Arnold, pleased nevertheless. 'I'm not that knowledgeable – not more than anyone else. I happened to have spent my formative years in one of Europe's most vibrant artistic centres.'

'It was Budapest, wasn't it?' chimes in Bertha, who likes to be seen as well travelled. 'I saw it in that article. I was going to ask you about it, Arnold. Have you been back there since – you know...?'

'No,' answers Arnold curtly. 'I haven't.'

'I don't mean to pry. It's just that I've been there – with Woolfie. It was the last trip we made together before he died. Prague, Vienna and Budapest. And do you know something, Arnold? I fell in *love* with

Budapest. Head over heels in love. I long to return there but – you know how it is... memories, memories...' She extracts a tissue from her handbag and dabs at the corners of her eyes.

'Don't Bertha,' says Helena. 'Don't upset yourself so.'

Bertha blows her nose. 'I'm sorry. I didn't mean to get soppy. After all, Budapest was – well, a happy place for Woolfie and me. For you, though, Arnold – I can't imagine what it would be like for you to return. You must have endured so much. In hiding, they said. How on earth did you manage to stay in hiding for so long?'

'It wasn't easy,' snaps Arnold. Surely the woman can tell that he is averse to this subject? What does one have to do to shut her up? Gag her?

Not with Helena around, good old Helena. Urging trout on the company, trout with almonds. And new potatoes and a colourful medley of vegetables steamed to perfection. Even Bertha is silenced, intent on her food, her zeal redirected from high art to gastronomy, her memory diverted from Woolfie's demise to former, glorious meals.

But Arnold cannot eat. He is disturbed again. His insides churn, his itch has returned and his spirits, unaccountably, have sunk lower than ever. He blames Bertha. No – it's pointless blaming her, she's stupid and ignorant. He blames Helena. She knows how he's feeling. How can she therefore have subjected him to this – this exposure, this discomfort? She ought to have protected him, kept him safe.

'I remember one particular night,' he says, without meaning to. What is he doing? Is this strange-sounding rumble his voice?

Silence falls over the dinner table. Everyone looks at him. Helena has paused in the distribution of broccoli and is regarding him with a puzzled frown. He averts his gaze.

'What happened?' asks Bertha. 'What do you remember?'

'It was a concert.' He has started and cannot stop. 'Jascha Heifetz was performing in the largest auditorium in Budapest – an enormous mirrored hall with notoriously bad acoustics. I'd only been in the city a few months and was enchanted by its glitter, its glamour. Everyone was there for the Heifetz concert – it was the highlight of the social calendar. I had very little money, but for this particular concert I'd scraped together the means to buy a ticket, the cheapest ticket…'

He pauses, massaging his forehead. Eating has been suspended. Everyone is listening intently.

'It was a cold night in March – March 1938. The atmosphere was highly charged – even at the back, right at the back, from where I strained to see the tiny blade-like figure of Heifetz on the platform. It didn't matter then that there was a discernible gap between the sound that drifted towards us and the movement on the stage.'

'A gap?' asks Bernard, who graduated from a minor conservatoire and considers himself an authority on musical terminology. 'Don't you perhaps mean a *rest*, Arnold?'

'*I* know what he means,' Bertha says, waving her knife eagerly. 'We must have been to the same hall, me and Woolfie. They played Strauss. I remember – *oom*-pa-pa, *oom*-pa-pa. The acoustics were so bad that when they were playing the pa-pa we were still hearing the *oom*.'

'At interval,' Arnold continues in a vague and dreamy manner, almost talking to himself, 'there was a buzz of excitement. As I made my way down the vast spiral staircase, I was almost swept off my feet by the crush. I thought at first that it was caused by the music, the occasion. Then I saw that newspapers were being passed from one group to another and people were straining to see the headlines.' He pauses. Everyone waits. 'At last I managed to see what the excitement was all about. Hitler had entered Vienna.'

'Goodness,' exclaims Maxine. 'That must have been chilling. I remember reading about…'

'Bells started ringing to announce that interval was over,' says Arnold, ignoring the interjection. 'Everyone trooped back to their seats and Heifetz went on playing as though nothing had happened. But I couldn't take my mind off those newspaper headlines. I didn't know much about Hitler, but there was something awful in the air, something dangerous. And it felt close, very close.'

'A premonition,' declares Bertha. 'You had a premonition.'

'Worse than that,' says Arnold. 'It was real fear – the sort that grabs you deep inside, constricts your chest and takes your breath away.' He speaks louder now, the remembered panic so vivid that it clutches him as though he were there again, crushed in the rear of that enormous auditorium. 'It became unbearable to be right at the back, so far away. I had to move forward, to push through the crowd towards the front where the rich people sat in their fine clothes. I thought I'd be safe with them. So I pressed forward and pressed forward, using my elbows and shoulders, ignoring the grumbling as I shoved people aside.'

His voice has become hoarse and unsteady with emotion. His hand is pressed against his chest, where he can feel tightness and dread.

'Arnold, take it easy.' Helena, who has been listening with frozen fascination, moves towards him and places a hand on his shoulder. He feels its warmth, but that doesn't seem to help.

'By the time the concert ended,' he gasps, 'I had reached the front... the very front.'

'Arnold,' says Helena, 'don't you think you ought to lie down?'

Limply he accedes, allowing her to take his arm and help him to his feet, to guide him to the door and slowly assist him upstairs. Every breath is an effort, every step is a stroke against an immensely powerful tide.

'Here we are,' she says at last. 'I'll help you take your shoes off. Try and relax.'

The dinner party resumes without him. From his bed Arnold hears random expressions of sympathy and concern infused with Helena's familiar verbal balm. 'Poor man... a difficult time... a certain age... the past...'

How far away it all sounds. A lifetime from the leafy boulevards, the wide promenades along the Danube. He remembers the cafés, the ice-rink in the city park. Budapest. Arnold aches still for the loss of it as acutely as he ached when he sensed that it was to be taken away.

16.

It was instant passion. That idiotic woman – how lightly she speaks about falling in love with Budapest, she and her God-awful Woolfie. What does she know? How can someone like her have any idea of that conviction of *rightness*, the thrill of discovery, the almost sexual tingle with which Arnold inhaled its culture and its effervescent beauty? How he revelled in those broad tree-lined streets, the shops, the coffee-houses, the conversation. I am here, he marvelled. I've arrived.

'I have to do this,' he told Rachel. 'You must understand. You *have* to understand.'

'I do,' she said, nursing the baby. Their baby. Their Miklós, who had entered the world puce-faced and wailing, an impossibly tiny creature she said was theirs. He didn't believe it. Couldn't. What could he have had to do with this alien limpet attached to her swollen breast?

From time to time he tried to touch it, to hold it. 'Miklós,' he whispered, as though by uttering its name he could personify it and care for it. Once, tentatively stroking the sleeping baby, he was beset by a stab of excruciating longing for something lost... a chicken, a mother, a childhood... But quickly he willed away the longing, for it was too painful to bear, and in its place came enormous rage. Fury strong enough to destroy this blindly trusting mite.

'It won't be for long, Rachel. I'll send for you soon.'

For some reason it seemed vital to leave with her blessing. He believed he wouldn't manage without her goodwill.

'Go, Arnost,' she said. 'Just go.' Her voice was gentle and resigned. He searched her face for any sign of bitterness or resentment. But no – she looked peaceful, cradling her baby. She seemed content.

Which gave him the courage to withstand the force of Yetta's disapproval and the potency of Hershel's suspicion.

'I don't understand why you can't stay here,' Yetta complained. 'Isn't Nyíregháza good enough for you?'

'It's not that,' protested Arnost. 'There are more opportunities in Budapest – better prospects, better jobs. I have contacts there – as soon as I'm established I'll send for Rachel and the baby. It will be a better life for them – much better than struggling along here.'

'And me?' Yetta asked. 'Do you think I want to live without my daughter or my grandson? What sort of life will it be for me?'

'You must come too,' declared Arnost. 'Of course you must. I wouldn't dream of sending for Rachel and Miklós without you.' He spoke with conviction but didn't dare meet her eyes. For Yetta was ill, very ill. Her breathlessness had become chronic and crippling. There was little chance that she'd survive the winter, never mind a move to Budapest. But that wasn't his fault, he told himself. He hadn't brought about the weakening of Yetta's lungs. Yetta wasn't his wife, after all, and his responsibility wasn't to her. It was to Rachel and the baby, and it was for their good, their future, that he was risking a solitary venture to Budapest.

'So,' Hershel said with dangerous irony in his voice. 'So, you're keeping your word.'

'What do you mean?' asked Arnost defensively.

'Exactly that. I am pleased to see that you are keeping your word.'

'What word? I'm not letting anyone down. I haven't broken any promises. I said I'd take care of Rachel – I married her, swore to look after her. What have I done that you should talk to me like this, what are you suggesting?'

'Nothing, nothing. Calm down, Arnost. I'm not suggesting anything.' He sighed, his particular, distinctive, infuriating sigh. Arnost resisted an impulse to smother him. Instead he launched into a long and passionate speech about being conscious of his duty, his sense of loyalty, the prosperity he would bring to his family by going to Budapest.

'I see,' responded Hershel dryly.

At which Arnost finally lost his temper. 'You?' he said with furious contempt. 'You don't see anything but those ridiculous Hebrew scratchings that have nothing at all to do with the real world. You're blind, Hershel. Half-witted and blind. You sit all day in that musty room with a crowd of no-hopers – *studying*, you say. Studying. Why aren't you living – doing – marrying? You're afraid, that's why. A coward.'

He watched with satisfaction as Hershel retreated from the force of his words and lowered himself into a chair, and sighed again and shook his head, and cradled it in his palms. 'So be it,' he said very softly. 'So be it.'

And suddenly, as though a knife were being plunged into his chest,

Arnost's satisfaction was supplanted by that terrible longing again – a distant memory of tenderness and love, a single instant when the two of them had seemed on the brink of understanding. He wanted to plead with Hershel. *Help me*, he wanted to say. Please will you help me?

A crazy impulse, he thought afterwards, when he had marched out of the house and into the town centre, where he toasted the future on local wine. How on earth, he wondered drunkenly, could a useless individual like Hershel Fine be of any assistance to someone as brave and intrepid as the fortune-seeking Arnost Rosenbaum?

He left Nyíregháza very soon after that. He'd assembled his meagre possessions – little more than he'd brought with him to Yetta's all those years before – in a battered and familiar-looking suitcase.

'Everything?' Rachel asked. 'You're taking everything?'

He kissed her on the cheek. 'It's not much,' he said, trying to sound nonchalant. 'I don't *have* much – *we* don't have much. But wait, Rachel. Give me a few months, just a few months.'

She silenced him, placing a finger across his lips. 'I know, Arnost. I understand. We'll wait. Miklós and I will wait.'

He turned away, for her forbearance made him uncomfortable. 'I'll write to you,' he said, lifting the suitcase and feeling its lightness and thinking how easy it would be to travel with a load so light. 'Take care of yourself – and Miklós. I'll write as soon as I've found somewhere to stay.'

He tried not to look back after saying goodbye. Walk on, he told himself. Walk on. But before he had reached the first corner something compelled him to glance over his shoulder.

And there she was, standing at the doorway, still. So very still, with the baby cleaving to her side. Arnost wrenched his gaze away, quickened his pace and did not stop till he reached the station. But despite all his efforts to concentrate on the journey and his promising future, the image of his wife and child had etched itself into his mind and haunted him all the way to Budapest.

Then he arrived, and any remorse was quickly obliterated by the wonder of the city. It was like a feast laid before a starving person. Tirelessly he trod from end to end. Greedily he grasped it, absorbed it and made it his. The buildings, the river, the Buda hills, the distant great plain. The cafés, where he listened to conversation so richly embellished and profound that he was rendered speechless, awestruck. Not for long, though, he resolved. Arnost Rosenbaum wouldn't stay silent for long.

He found work as a waiter in one of the elegant hotels overlooking the Danube. A temporary step. A necessary step. A perfect introduction to the life of the cultivated classes of Budapest.

While he waited, he watched. He watched the athletic contortions of his white-coated colleagues who balanced loaded trays above their heads on upturned palms. He heard them bragging that Hungarians could out-serve any other nationality. Let them out-serve, he thought scornfully. *They* would serve, but Arnost would *be* served. He had made up his mind about that. His fellow waiters didn't take to him, but he wasn't bothered. He overheard the names they called him. A typical Jew, one of them sneered, although Arnost had never spoken of his origins. A stinking Jew...

Haughtily he turned away – to those whose opinion of him would matter more than the envious ranting of the rank and file. It would be far more productive for him to impress and to emulate his customers, the gentry. While continuing to carry out his duties with sufficient diligence and efficiency to satisfy his employers, he embarked on his real education. It was a continuous and intensive vigil, the most important study course of his life.

Arnost had never been a true scholar. At school they had expected big things of him – but not as a reflection of his academic prowess. He had secured a place in the Gymnasium out of confidence and promise rather than his examination results, which were always mediocre. And in the end, when it came to the final tests for university, he had foundered. Yet that hadn't dampened his conviction that he was bound for success. Neither failure at school nor untimely fatherhood nor any other adversity had shaken his deep-seated certainty that ultimately he would find his niche, his true talent.

And he did. Not as a musician, an artist or a writer but as a man of refinement and breeding, a true son of Budapest. How quickly he learnt, how acutely he observed. How adept he proved at mastering the manners of the gentry – the way they handled their cutlery and sipped their drinks, their courtliness, their elegant style. He applied himself unflaggingly to his surveillance and then, in the privacy of his austere rented room, he practised and perfected. And read voraciously – not out of pleasure but with the specific intention of seasoning his conversation with allusions to the writer/poet/philosopher/musician of the day.

Until at last his probation paid off. When Sándor Novacek, one of the most important and influential customers at the hotel, invited Arnost to meet him for coffee at the Café New York, he wanted to hoot with triumph.

He didn't, naturally. He entered the palatial café as though he'd frequented such establishments all his life. Not for an instant did he reveal the thrill of blending his voice with the babble from a hundred marble tables and the melodies produced by the string orchestra in the gallery above. His eyes caressed the twisted marble columns and the ornate balustrade. He savoured his black coffee and made insightful comments about various celebrities, and knew he had come home.

Novacek, clearly impressed, invited him for lunch the following Sunday. 'My wife,' he said, 'would be honoured to meet you.'

Lunch? Arnost feigned a busy schedule and hesitated briefly. Novacek insisted and Arnost graciously accepted and (hiding his exultation) took down directions to the villa. As he did, he noted it was situated in one of the more exclusive areas of Budapest. It was on a hill overlooking the river, set in park-like grounds with an orchard of dwarf fruit trees.

'Do you like it?' inquired Madame Novacek, noticing his rapt admiration of the view from the veranda.

'It's wonderful. Unbelievable!'

For days afterwards snatches of conversation lingered in his head. He felt as though he were on the brink of something marvellous – like Aladdin at the entrance to the open cave. Soon the treasure would be his.

Like the Novaceks, he'd buy his cheese from the same shop as the Habsburgs and display his homegrown dwarf fruit in lead crystal bowls.

Such a sense of infinite possibilities! And very quickly endorsed when Sándor Novacek, who happened to own one of the largest textile manufacturing companies in Hungary, offered Arnost a clerical job in his Budapest headquarters. It was very far from an appointment to the Board. But the white-coated waiter was now a white-collar worker – and then? Who knew? 'You're an enterprising young man, Arnost,' said Novacek. 'I have an instinct about you – a feeling you'll go far.'

That night Arnost celebrated. Up and down the boulevards, from café to café, drunk not on alcohol but on achievement and the certainty of success. Nothing would stand in his way. Rumours of war? Nothing to do with him. Legislation against Jews? He'd deny it, deny his Jewishness, no one would know, how could they? His wife? His son? He brushed aside their existence. Pushed it away. That was in another life, a completely different life – he'd been young and stupid. Nyíregháza had become a distant memory, tiny and irrelevant.

So he told himself. But when he returned to his rented room after his celebrations, he was suddenly acutely lonely. He longed for someone with whom to share his success and, for the first time in several weeks, wrote to Rachel:

> ...Have patience, I'll send for you soon – you and Miklós...

Did he mean what he wrote? Was there a shred of sincerity in his oft-repeated words? How does one evaluate years later, decades later, the measure of responsibility, the extent of treachery – if there *was* any treachery? Surely a young man so bewitched by Budapest could not be held responsible for his actions? He hadn't asked for dependants, after all. All he wanted – and he'd had little enough in his life – was a chance. Novacek had given it to him and he intended to grasp hold of it with all his might.

> ...The important thing is to get myself established. I'm sure you can understand that....

Of course she would. She always had. Hershel... perhaps not. But what did Hershel know? What had he ever done? Could Hershel – in the face of anti-Jewish laws and economic recession and escalating war-phobia – have found himself a position in a powerful international company? Could *he* have become the favourite, the pet, of one of the most influential families in Budapest?

> ...I have made friends with a very nice family called Novacek. The husband, Sándor, has become my employer and is most kind to me – I have had several meals at his home and he gives me concert tickets when he can. He has an elegant wife and two very plain daughters...

The older, Olga, was particularly plain – and desperately seeking a male admirer. Arnost hugely enjoyed flirting with her, putting into practice all the gallant flourishes he'd so diligently acquired. Kissing her hand, clicking his heels, adorning his conversation with soulful sighs and poetic flourishes. He executed all this with such smooth proficiency that one would have imagined he'd been born to it. Arnost himself had begun to believe this to be so.

Or half-believe. Maybe even three-quarters, possibly nine-tenths. But there was a crack – a tiny opening into a recess deep inside. It was the place where he had tried to seal his earliest and most tender memories – the place where he'd felt pain on touching Miklós, on deriding Hershel, on leaving Rachel. He assumed that if he starved this place, denied it food or light or air, it would shrivel and die. But then, just when he would be almost sure that was no longer a gap, something would happen to remind him of its presence.

The news of Yetta's death, for instance. 'It was awful,' wrote Rachel. 'She gasped for every last breath. Her final words were that I must go to Budapest as soon as you send for me. A child needs a father, she said.'

He read it again and again. A child needs a father, a child needs a father. Pain shot through him, bringing tears to his eyes. But he blinked them away and ordered himself not to cry. To be strong...

Strong enough to fight his way to the front of the auditorium on the night of the much-vaunted Heifetz concert – the night he heard that Germany had entered Austria, the night he was filled with deep and irrational fear and decided that whatever happened he could survive.

The next day, though, something happened to shake his resolve. He had accompanied the lumpy Olga Novacek to the National Gallery and was midway through an exposition on Romantic Eclecticism when his eye fell on a painting of the Virgin and Child. He stopped. Olga looked puzzled, unable to understand why Arnost's eloquent prattle had ceased. 'What's wrong?' she asked.

For a moment he was unable to formulate an answer. He couldn't shift his gaze. Instead of the bland face of the artist's Mary, he saw Rachel. Rachel with baby Miklós, just as on the day he had left Nyíregháza. Her expression was one of utter devotion, single-minded absorption in the small being who was cradled in her arms, placidly asleep.

The pain that tore through him nearly caused Arnost to cry out aloud. Almost immediately, though, he recovered. 'Come,' he said, taking Olga's arm and steering her as far as possible from the image that had so disturbed him. As though nothing had happened, he resumed his discourse.

That evening he kissed Olga. He forced himself to do it out of defiance – as a challenge to the wife who was haunting him and the baby son whose helplessness was upsetting him. 'Dear, dear Olga,' he crooned.

'Oh, Arnost...'

Their lips met and for an instant he forget that the mouth against his was that of poor dull Olga. He found himself aroused, pressing against her, almost choking with desire.

But then he became aware of an alien presence, something cold brushing against him and a voice whispering in his ear: 'A child needs a father – a child needs a father.'

'Go away! Leave me alone, will you? Leave me in peace!'

Someone is touching him – there's a hand on his shoulder. He shakes it away.

'Arnold?'

'Let me be, for God's sake. Won't you please let me be?'

'They've gone, Arnold.'

'Who?' He opens his eyes and sees that Helena is perched at the side of the bed still in her dinner-party finery.

'The guests, of course... Arnold, you've been perspiring – you're wet through. Are you feeling any better? You gave us all quite a turn, you know.'

'It was nothing,' he says weakly.

'Well, we're not about to take any chances. I'm not happy about you, not happy at all. First thing tomorrow we're off to the doctor, you and me. And if Malcolm can't fit you in, someone else will.'

17.

Malcolm is unable to see Arnold the next day. 'He's fully booked until Thursday,' reports Helena after a lengthy altercation with the receptionist. 'At least that's what she insists. Between us, though, I think he's off playing golf.' She pours their tea.

Reprieved, thinks Arnold, unsure how or why he has come up with this particular word. His head feels thick, his mental lexicon unreachable. 'No matter,' he says, so mildly that Helena stops pouring to stare at him in puzzlement.

'No *matter*?' she repeats. '*You're* the one who's been saying for weeks how you need to see a doctor.'

'Thursday will do.' Arnold hopes she'll let the issue be and allow him the space, the four extra days. Although he believes there is nothing serious amiss, the delay is a relief. A remission.

'Thursday *won't* do.' Helena drops two sweetening tablets into her tea and stirs it purposefully. 'This is not what we've been paying insurance for all these years. If Malcolm sets himself up as a private GP, he ought to deliver the goods. Never before have I had to ask for an urgent appointment.'

'I don't *need* an urgent appointment.'

'I do,' she says. 'For my peace of mind. I've been very worried about you, Arnold, and last night put the cap on it. Everyone was saying – you should have heard them – how one can't be too vigilant, medically speaking. Bertha told us about this friend she'd met on the QE2 – a man your age, I believe...'

He is never to learn the fate of Bertha's shipmate (not a happy-ever-after tale, he suspects), for the telephone rings and Helena, after a monosyllabic dialogue, turns to him in triumph. 'He'll see you! I knew they would come back to me. I gave them a piece of my mind.'

'Malcolm's found a space?' asks Arnold with a sinking sensation.

'No, his partner. A new doctor called Fowles. They say he's very good – extremely bright. He'll see you at twelve.'

Arnold wants to put his foot down, to refuse to be examined by anyone other than Malcolm. After all these years, he resents being looked at by anyone else and shouldn't be expected to subject himself to someone new. But before he can say anything, extreme fatigue takes hold. A kind of limp passivity which he has never before experienced. As though he is no longer in charge... as though he has given over the driving seat to Helena... to fate... to bright new Dr Fowles.

Who frowns in disbelief when he has taken Arnold's blood pressure. 'One moment,' he says as he reinflates the arm tube. 'I'll need to do that again to make sure.'

'Is it bad?' asks Arnold apprehensively. He is aware of a thudding through his arteries, a beat throbbing from his arm to his chest and echoing in his pounding head.

'*Bad* is not a word we like to use in this context,' says Dr Fowles when he has concluded his second reading. 'We're talking about a measurement here. A scale. Naturally, we have a range we consider within the bounds of normality, but it doesn't necessarily mean that those who fall outside those limits...'

'Please,' interrupts Arnold, who is becoming increasingly uneasy. Malcolm usually glances at his psoriasis and hands out a prescription while engaged in amiable banter. Not this young upstart. He insists on a thorough examination, despite Arnold's assertion that a sound constitution like his doesn't need digging and delving. He isn't a guinea pig, after all. On the other hand, if the examination has revealed something, he'd prefer the idiot to come to the point. 'Would you tell me what you have found?'

'Right,' says Dr Fowles, 'I'll be simple and direct. The point is that your blood pressure seems to be much higher than even the highest levels of normality. To put it bluntly, I fear for the condition of your heart.' He pauses to leaf through Arnold's records. 'I don't know how long this has been going on for – I see that the last time you had your blood pressure checked was... nine, ten years ago?'

'For my insurance medical,' says Arnold stiffly. 'I was found to be in perfect health.'

'Good,' says the doctor, continuing to read the notes. 'It's as well to have insurance. Sporadic psoriasis... oh, you mentioned that, didn't you? And chronic insomnia. Too much medication – *far* too much. Anyway, we'll attend to all that as soon as we've got your circulatory system sorted out. Now – before we do anything else, I'd like to take an ECG.'

'A – what?' asks Arnold, trying to sound nonchalant. He has never paid much attention to the workings of his vital organs, simply trusting them to get on with it. Now, suddenly, he discovers that all the while a torrential and relentless river of blood has been bombarding his heart. And if that isn't enough, this doctor is shaking his head like a plumber surveying the mess made by the last person on the job and bemusing Arnold with jargon. The boy probably wasn't even born when Arnold first started seeing Malcolm.

'An electrocardiogram,' he explains, carefully and kindly, as though talking to a cretin. 'It will give us some idea of how much your heart has been affected. Once we've got that done, we'll ask Mrs Rose to join us and we can decide what to do next.'

Helena is wearing her pinched, fraught face when she enters the surgery, having spent a few minutes chatting privately with Dr Fowles. Who has,

Arnold is sure, furnished her with graphic enlightenment on her husband's physical state. She draws a chair alongside his and reaches out for his hand. He pulls it away. With any encouragement, she'll lapse into hospice-volunteer mode, and things are bad enough without that.

The doctor meanwhile is studying a series of zig-zagging graphs from one angle, then another. 'It's not good,' he says at last. 'The heart seems to be seriously enlarged.'

'Enlarged?' repeats Helena, while Arnold imagines his vastly distended organ pulsating in his chest. He can feel it pressing against his breastbone and pushing up into his throat. Will it burst? *Can* it burst? He swallows hard and breathes deeply, telling himself sternly to employ some self-control.

'An exercise ECG,' Dr Fowles is saying, 'is probably what we need next. I'm going to refer you to a cardiologist, Mr Rose. An excellent man. Dr Terence Irving. I'll mark the case urgent, so you should be hearing from him very soon.'

They return home in silence. Arnold finds it hard to believe that this very same day they made the appointment and travelled in bright sunshine into Harley Street. Is he the same person who arrogantly dismissed any sign of ill-health – who had unshakeable confidence in the workings of his body? Dangerously high blood pressure? A greatly enlarged heart? Surely not Arnold Rose, with his foresight and energy?

'You'd better rest,' says Helena when they reach the house. 'You heard what Dr Fowles said about taking things easy until the specialist gets in touch.'

'I heard.' Arnold sinks wearily on to the sofa and shuts his eyes. He doesn't mind resting. In fact it's a relief to have a legitimate excuse to relax. He'll take advantage of the situation while it lasts. Without doubt, this Dr Irving will do his exercise test (whatever that means) and conclude that the Fowles fellow is a bumbling fool and the whole thing is a mistake. It will be quite satisfying to confront him with his ineptitude and perhaps consider taking legal action. Meanwhile, though, he'll make the most of his short-term status as an invalid.

He doesn't realise until it's too late that his submission to the role of patient has propelled Helena into the role of carer. 'It's your diet,' she declares, bustling into the sitting room just as Arnold is dropping off. 'I'm sure it is. Haven't I been begging you for years to go easy on fats? It was the first thing they told Norman Wilson after he had that coronary a few years ago – not that you've had a coronary – but Betty says…'

'You've spoken to Betty already?' he asks, more mildly than he would normally have done. If he were feeling himself he would undoubtedly have made some caustic comment about Helena's compulsion to share the minutiae of their lives with her bunch of acolytes. He'd have insisted on discretion. But now her garrulousness seems irrelevant.

'She happened to phone, so I mentioned it. Without going into details, of course. Anyway, we don't know the extent of the damage yet. We won't until we hear from… oh, by the way, Betty says that Terence Irving is absolutely top notch. He treated Norman and look at him today.'

'Look at him,' says Arnold dryly.

'His brother Marcus is the osteopath everyone's raving about. In fact, he's the man Lily Sanderson's been seeing. He manipulates her neck.'

'I see.' Even in extremis Arnold experiences a shudder of abhorrence at the mention of Lily, but rather likes the idea of someone applying pressure to her neck.

'Which reminds me,' continues Helena. 'I ought to phone Lily. She must have been in unbearable pain to miss one of my dinner parties. Let me give her a quick ring to find out how she is – I'll be back in a tick.'

Before he can object, she is out of the room and on the line to Lily. Despite his efforts not to listen (for he's been warned to avoid all possible sources of stress), he can hear cluckings of sympathy and then – predictably – the sober-voiced communication of Arnold's condition. Stop it, he wants to say. Stop it *now*. But how can they? It's prime material, to be scrutinised from every perspective – causes, treatment, ultimate prognosis.

Then, just as it seems the conversation is entering its final stages, there's a complete change of tone. '*Really*?' he hears Helena exclaim.

'How amazing! What a coincidence... he'll be so astonished. I'll tell him right away.'

Fear grips Arnold. It's irrational, he knows. They are probably shrieking about some aspect of their museum or exchanging gossip about the Cantor, or intrigue in one of their sub-committees. There's no need – he tells himself – for this dread that is making his bowels churn, his heart pound, and his head spin. No need at all. Yet as Helena's footsteps approach, their eager click-clicking on the parquet floor getting nearer and nearer, Arnold's terror grows so intense that he almost faints.

'You'll never guess, Arnold,' she says, out of breath.

'What?' he forces himself to ask, managing somehow to produce a sound that simulates his speaking voice. His dizziness is profound. If he weren't already recumbent on the sofa, he would have to lie down.

'Lily tells me...' She suddenly notices his pallor and shortness of breath. 'Goodness, Arnold – you look dreadful. I think I'm going to phone Dr Irving and demand an immediate appointment. We can't afford to wait.'

'No, leave it, Helena,' he manages, desperate to harness this galloping drama. He wants time... to catch his breath, to think. No – not to think. He doesn't want to think.

'Well...' she says doubtfully. 'Anyway – this will cheer you up.' She pauses dramatically, as though about to produce a gift. 'Lily got the most delightful letter from that Hershel – the synagogue caretaker, remember?'

He nods, poised for the worst. But now that it's happening, it doesn't seem as bad as he expected. Like his apprehension about flying: once the plane accelerates for take-off, there is nothing to be done and fear seems pointless.

'He sent his best wishes to you – on your retirement.'

'To me?' stalls Arnold.

'Yes – he says he recognised you from that piece in the *JC*. You and he were quite close, so he claims.'

'Close?' Arnold splutters, for the word causes his skin to crawl and his stomach to contract again. Close... closeness. The closeness welded by the shedding of the last of his boyhood tears, the closeness denied by betrayal. 'He's mad.' Arnold is shocked by the harshness of his tone, but he has to say something, he must respond. 'He's mad – senile – completely off his head.'

18.

Is Hershel mad? This is what Ms Valerie Fallon is currently trying to establish. Of course, Ms Fallon – an Outreach Social Worker employed by the Menorah Retirement Consortium – would never put it so crudely. Her mission, as she has explained to Hershel, is to administer the routine 'mini mental test' required for entrance into all Menorah Homes.

'You mean,' ponders Hershel, who has admitted her into his flat with extreme reluctance, 'you want to see maybe if I'm too crazy to fit into your deluxe establishment – God forbid a lunatic should slip into such a fancy place.'

'No, no, Mr Fine – it's not like that at all.' With practised deftness she has manoeuvred herself further into the flat and, once she has settled in a chair, extracts from her briefcase a folder and a fountain pen. 'The purpose of my visit is to assess your level of competence – of social adaptability. You see, the residents of the Menorah form a close and harmonious group – a family, if you like. It wouldn't be fair on them to introduce a non-conformist. Not that I'm suggesting...'

She's suggesting nothing, yet her pen is already scratching away with what Hershel is sure must be evidence of his unsuitability. So what. A family like that he neither asked for nor needed. And what questions she's asking! An insult. Name the Queen. Name the Prime Minister. Name the month we're in.

'This is an outrage,' he explodes at last, having countered her interrogation with silence and a stony stare. 'What am I – a criminal with a record, that you should be checking up on me like this? Never mind – wait till I start checking up on *you*, Miss...'

'Fallon – Val, if you like. Look, Mr Fine, no one has suggested that you're in any way disreputable. On the contrary, your employers have given you a *wonderful* letter of reference. What we're trying to establish is whether you'll integrate at Menorah, that's all.'

'And for that I must mention the name of Her Majesty the Queen? A recommendation from the synagogue chairman isn't enough?'

'You're misunderstanding me. It was a simple general knowledge question. I certainly didn't mean to overtax or upset you.'

'Upset? Me *upset*? This, my dear lady, is not the way Hershel Fine acts upset. You want upset? I'll give you upset.'

'No, no – please.' She retreats to her folder, her pen scratching away. Paranoia. Hysteria. Transient confusion. 'Mr Fine, I didn't *volunteer* to administer this evaluation. I was sent here. It's my job.'

'And so?'

'So will you try and make it easier? For both of us?'

He shrugs. 'Pity you should have such a difficult time,' he mutters sarcastically.

'Tell you what,' she says with over-eager desperation, 'let's put aside the general knowledge and move on to something else... something simpler, perhaps. Could you possibly give me a brief description of this room?'

'Could you possibly give me a brief description of this room?' Hershel mimics with a simper. He is deeply offended now. Crazy is one thing, but for this smug little creature to imply that he is either blind or senile is beyond a joke. 'How can you call this luxurious chamber a mere *room*? Take a look at the chandelier, my friend – the Persian rugs, the antiques, the paintings, the...'

'Mr Fine,' she interrupts, adding 'deluded' to her diagnosis, 'that's enough, thank you. The next thing to consider is your numeracy – just *basic* numeracy, of course. We're not asking for Einstein.' She gives a small dry laugh.

'Why not?' demands Hershel. 'Not even Einstein is good enough for you?'

Ignoring this, she concentrates intently on her questionnaire. Enunciating very slowly and clearly she says: 'Would you please subtract seven from thirty?'

'Seven what?'

'Seven *anything*, Mr Fine – anything at all.'

'What are you talking about – anything? By me, seven is an important number, one of the most important. Seven are the days of Creation, the days in the week, the wonders of the world. As for thirty – who knows thirty? Thir*teen*, on the other hand – thirteen are God's attributes. Twelve are the tribes of Israel, eleven the stars in Joseph's dream, ten the Commandments, nine the months of childbearing...'

'I give up,' she breaks in, and shuts her folder decisively. 'You are clearly not taking this seriously. I'm going to have to talk to Management about your attitude. Most people would be *grateful* for an opportunity such as the one being offered to you.' She rises to her feet and packs away her implements.

Hershel meanwhile stands up and awaits her departure with exaggerated courtliness and his most beguiling smile. He enjoys her bewilderment as she prepares to bid farewell to a raving lunatic but sees instead an amiably polite white-haired gentleman. 'Good day,' he says courteously, opening the door.

She collects herself. Her lips tighten. 'You'll be hearing from us soon, Mr Fine,' she says ominously.

The door shuts decisively and Hershel rubs his hands together in glee. He's in a better mood than he has been for weeks. It has struck him that there is enormous power in being old beyond caring. Poor girl, so superior she thinks she is with her papers and idiotic questions – and meanwhile Hershel calls the shots. 'It's my job.' Such self-importance. Such frustration because Hershel is making this great job so *difficult* for her. Let her try maybe half-an-hour in a copper-mine – fifteen minutes even – and she'd come running back, begging for the delightful task of cross-examining Hershel Fine.

Who will always hold the upper hand because he simply isn't interested in the outcome of the interrogation. Does it *matter* where they put him to reach the end of his days? Is he *bothered* whether it's in this flat or the street or in a glass case or a bed in the sumptuous Menorah Home?

He chortles to himself as he remembers his fulsome description of this austere room. A bitter joke, he thinks. A person should cry, not laugh.

But that would be a problem, for Hershel does not cry. He's not proud of this. On the contrary, he knows that, according to the sages, the Lord is quite partial to tears. He's aware that when all other heavenly gates are shut, the Gate of Tears remains open. But that's no comfort to him, for he has lost the ability to weep. Not one single tear has he ever shed for those he lost. He can sigh, he can talk – and laugh – and even pray. But with the death of his loved ones went his capacity to cry.

Does Arnold cry, he wonders, returning to his preoccupation with the man who, these days, is never far from his mind. Hershel remembers the single instance when he witnessed young Arnost weeping. But now – now that he's transformed himself into the great Mr Rose...? For years Hershel believed that Arnost had perished in the War – not that this would have brought Rachel back, but somehow it squared things and made them more possible to understand.

Now it appears that, far from being dead, Arnost has become a prosperous and respected member of society. Even so, Hershel has tried to convince himself that although it doesn't seem fair (but who ever said that life was fair?), one cannot deny a person's right to try and overcome what was, for all of them, a terrible time. Anyway, who knows what suffering Arnost endured? Who knows how deeply he mourned?

Hershel knows. No one has told him, but he knows with certainty that the person called Arnold Rose has shed every vestige of his former existence. No wonder he did so well – he carried no luggage, nothing to impede him. Hershel, on the other hand, came here with a burden and has borne it ever since. And what a heavy load it has been.

But now he is determined to share it. Why should he drop like a rock into his grave while lofty Mr Rose trips in as light as a gazelle? Not that Hershel is judging the man, for who is he to say that carrying the past is a virtue and travelling light a great vice? There is Another, better equipped to pass judgement. With Arnost's luck, though, he'll manage somehow to slide into the Great Leviathan Feast while Hershel is excluded on account of failing some mini mental test.

Ah well. Nothing to be done. Hershel is too old and tired to think about revenge. All he wants is to nudge Arnost's memory a little – remind him maybe that a Kaddish or two for his late wife and child wouldn't be amiss. With this in mind, he wonders whether Lily Sanderson has passed on his greetings and desire for a reunion.

He finds out the next day when Lily arrives at his door. She is wearing a yellow spring frock and a surgical neck collar.

'What happened?' Hershel is aghast. It's his first encounter with an orthopaedic restraint of this magnitude.

'Oh – just a few upper vertebrae,' says Lily casually, watching for his reaction.

'That's all?' asks Hershel, taking her nonchalance at face value. 'It looks serious.'

'It *is* serious,' she confirms. 'Fortunately I'm blessed with a brilliant osteopath.'

'Very lucky for you.' Hershel is unsure about the function of an osteopath but marvels at the range of benedictions available to mankind. How many has he missed through leading such a narrow life?

'Enough about me,' says Lily, bestowing on him a dazzling smile to convey her bravery under the circumstances. 'I came here to talk about you.' Before Hershel has time to object she has pushed past him into the flat and tidied the kitchen and swept the floor and made tea. 'And here,' she says, catching her breath and holding forth a small dish in which she has placed a single jam doughnut. 'I brought this for you. I thought it would make you feel better.'

Hershel accepts it warily. 'There's nothing wrong with *me*,' he points out. 'You should be having it.'

'Me?' She shudders as theatrically as her neck-gear allows. 'It's the last thing I need. Marcus – he's the osteopath I mentioned – has threatened to stop treating me unless I lose weight. Without him, God knows where I'd be.'

Not interfering in my life for a start, thinks Hershel cruelly.

'Eat,' she urges. 'Go on – enjoy yourself.'

He chews and swallows obediently under her avid gaze, wishing she would move to the real purpose of her visit. He feels unable to raise the subject himself. 'And so?' he manages at last, having licked the last grain of sugar from his thumb.

'So.' She drains her cup slowly. 'It's not looking good.'

'What?' he asks with trepidation.

'Arnold.'

'Arnold,' he repeats. There – he has uttered it. His name. Now that it's out in the open, he feels empowered to talk. 'You mentioned what I wrote to you about meeting Arnold?'

'Of course – I told Helena, his wife, and she was thrilled about the idea of a reunion. There's a problem, though.'

'Oh, yes?' Naturally, thinks Hershel. Did he imagine Arnost would make it *easy* for a confrontation? He'll do everything possible to slip out of Hershel's grasp. 'What's the problem?'

'He's not well.' Her voice is low and confidential, and when she sees Hershel's disbelieving face she touches his arm. 'Between us,' she whispers, 'I don't think he's well at all.'

'To me he looked in peak condition,' he says, shrugging her away.

'Appearances are nothing,' she declares. 'You should have seen my cousin Philip a fortnight before he died – no one would have dreamed... a young man too. Far younger than Arnold.'

'What's the problem?'

'With Philip it was liver cancer.'

'With Arnold?'

'Blood pressure. Sky-high. I wouldn't say this to Helena, but I hope he's made a will. Not that there isn't treatment for that sort of condition, but my belief is that with Arnold's past he won't last long... especially now that they've found his heart is so enlarged.'

'You're telling me he's likely to – die?' Hershel is suddenly, unaccountably, gripped by an ache. Is he upset, then, for the imminent demise of someone he has cursed for as long as he can remember – someone he once gladly wrote off as dead? Surely he's not about to grieve for a stranger called Arnold Rose? Yet his sadness is undeniable. 'Oh, my,' is all he can say.

'I knew you'd be concerned,' says Lily with satisfaction. 'That's why I came here to break it to you gently. But what can one do?' She bounces to her feet and gathers the teacups and returns to the kitchen where she resumes her domestic zeal. When she reappears after a furious bout of clinking and splashing, Hershel wonders whether he is expected to applaud. He rises to his feet in relieved anticipation of her final exit – but no, it seems she has further business to discuss. She settles back on her chair.

'That leaves us,' she says, conspiratorially.

'Us?' Hershel asks. Is she suggesting an affair?

'I've decided that in the absence of Arnold we should concentrate on making an aural history.'

Hershel stares at her in astonishment. What does she mean? Never mind an affair, he and Lily Sanderson are going to make *history*?

'Let me explain,' she says eagerly. 'You're going to tell me about your experiences and I'll tape your account. I'll ask you questions from time to time to jog your memory. Mostly though, it will be *your* story – a valuable addition to our archives. Think about it – when your generation disappears we'll have no access at all to the kind of experiences you had. The concentration camps, for instance.'

He stops her. 'Hold it there – wait a second, Mrs Sanderson.'

'I understand,' she says sorrowfully. 'I know how difficult this is going to be. I can imagine how awful it was in – Auschwitz, was it? Or was it Belsen?'

'Neither.'

'Oh? Well, then…'

'Mrs Sanderson…'

'Lily, please.'

'Lily – I'm sorry to disappoint you but I wasn't in a concentration camp.'

'You *weren't*?' She looks bewildered. 'But I thought… it's what everyone says.'

19.

They can say what they like – embellish, embroider, stand on their heads if they want to – but that doesn't change the truth. Hershel Fine has neither claimed nor experienced the dubious distinction of imprisonment in a concentration camp. He remembers once being included in a gathering of survivors who were dropping with an air of superiority the name of the terrible camp they had endured. One would have thought they'd applied for the place and then graduated with honours – Oxford and Auschwitz, the same.

'How about you?' they asked Hershel. 'In which camp were you?'

They exchanged glances when he told them. They raised their eyebrows. A *labour* camp? Ought Hershel to be included in their ranks? Putting it frankly: Did he suffer enough?

Hershel wonders why some people believe they have a monopoly on suffering – and why they think there is virtue in it. Did those who suffered most (if one could measure such things) acquire moral superiority? Did they emerge cleaner and whiter – like laundry after a vigorous boil-wash? As far as Hershel noticed, people remained people – good, bad, usually a bit of both. Most lived unremarkable lives, transcended by the instances of nobility that gave Hershel hope. They were little people – heartbreakingly frail compared with the might of history – who were trapped in the vortex of big times. Some clung on tenaciously but in vain. Others simply let go and were swept away by the current. Of the latter, there were those who were cast ashore and saved. All random. The indiscriminate workings of chance. Nothing at all to do with morality.

Those whom chance favoured – or not, for Hershel has often thought survival to be more a curse than a blessing – resumed their fractured life. They had to plaster their wounds (as though there's any balm for wounds so deep) and take the tentative steps of a convalescent. A permanent convalescent, who would tread with the utmost caution to the end of his allotted span. Never again trusting in the ordinariness of drawing breath – or having children – or mundane good-neighbourliness. Always afraid that big times, like black thunderclouds, would gather and strike again. And jealous. Jealous of their badge of suffering – the concentration camp number stamped indelibly on their arm. Jealous of this pedigree of endurance, for it is often the only thing they have.

Hershel came through without even a label. A copper mine in Yugoslavia? Who has ever heard of that? Certainly not do-gooding Lily Sanderson whose disappointed face falls almost through her neck-brace when he tries to explain. No – the axe that crashed down and severed Hershel's life didn't even boast the distinction of notoriety.

Two lives. Before the axe and afterwards. Peering back through the smokescreen of his tragedy, Hershel perceives the time before as idyllic – knowing full well that it seemed far from perfect then.

Whatever the difficulties, though, they were precious days. He was with Rachel, taking care of her and the child. She kept insisting it was a temporary situation – it wouldn't be long before they joined Arnost in Budapest. Hershel didn't believe it for a moment.

'He's found a job in a textile company,' she announced one day. 'It won't be long now.'

'Don't get too excited,' was Hershel's response. He didn't want to dampen her optimism, but the truth was the truth. Arnost was clearly gulping down the excitement of the big city, doing well, making important friends. Only a saint would want a wife and child round his neck in such a situation – and Arnost was no saint. If Rachel hadn't been in such a hurry, Hershel would have matched her with a saint in the Yeshiva.

'He *will* send for us.' Rachel's face was set. She insisted on Arnost's devotion to the last. 'If he doesn't, we'll go and find him. You must get married, Hershel. You can't devote your entire life to us. Rivke won't wait forever.'

Hershel didn't answer. He had discovered the previous day that good, stoical Rivke, to whom he had been betrothed since boyhood and who had been on patient standby while Hershel discharged his family duties, was biding her time no longer. Her marriage to another had been announced. He was sad but not bitter. How could one regret the time devoted to Rachel? And how could he for an instant begrudge a single moment of closeness with his nephew Miklós?

Even now when Hershel thinks of Miklós he is assailed by a wave of grief that almost makes him sob aloud. If he ever cries again, it will be for the love and loss of his sister's child. He watched Miklós grow from infancy to inquisitive boyhood, celebrating the joy of his achievements, the marvel of his existence. With mixed feelings he would hear Rachel telling her son tales of bravery and virtue and fidelity. The hero of most of these stories was his noble father Arnost, who had gone to Budapest to make their fortune.

'Tell it to me again,' the child would insist. He never tired of it. Nor did Rachel seem to tire of reiterating her husband's virtues.

Did she believe what she was saying? Did she somehow imagine that repetition would make the stories true? Hershel doesn't know – he has never known, for, with Rachel, the subject of Arnost was strictly out of bounds. He had no doubt that she loved him, though, for better or worse. Hers was an undemanding devotion that made infinite allowances.

'A child needs a father,' Yetta whispered, her last words, and Rachel wept tears that Hershel suspected were not entirely for her dying mother. Immediately after the week of mourning, the *shiva* during which they sat and wept on low stools, she faced Hershel with new determination.

'I'll write to him today,' she said, 'and tell him that the time has come. It's been far too long. I'll demand that he either comes home or arranges for us to go to Budapest as soon as possible.'

She wrote, but Hershel didn't know how strongly she phrased her letter. He knew that, a year later, there they were still waiting.

Then the axe fell. In February 1943 came the news that the German government had ordered the Hungarian authorities to send 10,000 Jews to work as forced labourers in the copper mines at Bor in Yugoslavia. Who argued with the Germans? They dictated and Hungary supplied. A few months later, while 75,000 Hungarian Jews remained untouched and still in ignorance of their fate, 10,000 were transported to labour camps.

Including Hershel.

It happened so quickly that he had no time to reflect or even to say goodbye properly. Anyway, who knew what would happen – who could have guessed? In other parts of Europe, Jews were already being slaughtered left, right and centre – but in Hungary they felt safe. Hershel had no sense of doom about his departure to the copper mines. Hard work never killed anyone. So he thought.

Other matters concerned him more – even then. He still felt acutely the absence of his mother and worried about how his sister and nephew would manage during his (temporary) absence. Most of all, though, his mind remained engaged in the Great Imponderables that the Hebrew sages had not yet deciphered but would surely be resolved by brilliant Hershel Fine.

Even then.

'Take care of yourself,' he urged Rachel when he departed. 'Take care of Miklós. Let Arnost know that I've had to go away. I'm sure that when he finds out you're alone…'

He spoke with confidence, to reassure her and also because he wanted to believe it himself. But as soon as the train drew out of Nyíregháza, he was filled with dread. It travelled with him on the interminable journey, accompanying him on the march to the camp and on his confrontation with his harsh new surroundings. It was his constant companion through his physical trials, even harder to bear than the pain and the hunger. The only antidote to the dread was Hershel's abiding belief that God would take care of them.

Even then.

Like counterweights in his consciousness were the two opposing forces: dread on the one side and belief on the other. When Hershel almost succumbed to dread, belief would dominate and he would resume his labours with renewed conviction that Rachel and Miklós would be awaiting him when his trials ended.

He was wrong, of course.

Or maybe God was wrong.

Meanwhile here's Lily Sanderson visibly disappointed because Hershel's story, his aural history, doesn't feature a show-stopping camp. She isn't despondent for long, though. 'Even if you *weren't* in Auschwitz or Belsen,' she says encouragingly, 'I'd still like to hear about it. What I'd *really* like would be to tape you and Arnold Rose together, since you said that you and he were close. I do hope he makes a recovery, even if it's only temporary.'

Hershel nods, his mind miles and decades absent. He wishes the woman would take her false compassion and ugly neck-brace away. He wants solitude. He needs to think. Distractedly, he accepts the sheet of notepaper she hands him and sees that it is Arnold Rose's address and telephone number. His immediate impulse is to hand it straight back to her. Instead, he finds himself inserting it into his pocket.

'By the way,' she is saying, 'I wrote *another* letter to Natie Goldfarb about your eviction. A strong letter – one that they can't ignore. We'll win this, Hershel!'

Deep fatigue assails him. 'I've told you several times that it doesn't matter.'

'Of course it matters. I refuse to let them walk roughshod over you. We're up against fascism here.'

Fascism? She thinks *this* is fascism? How on earth can he force her to leave? 'I've decided that I *want* to go to the Menorah,' he says in a flash of inspiration. 'A very nice lady came here to see me and told me what a wonderful place it is – friendly people, excellent food, beautifully decorated. So I thought to myself – why not? She says I'll fit in like a glove.'

'Well…' Lily sounds doubtful and disappointed. 'If that's what you want.'

'It is. Definitely.'

Hershel draws himself to his feet and she has no option but to do likewise. When she has finally departed, with much fussing and displacement of air, he wants to scream out his relief. He paces the room with his hands in his pockets – and extracts the sheet with Arnold's address. Arnold Rose. Sick Arnold Rose. Dying Arnold Rose.

But Arnold Rose is immortal, Hershel tells himself. He's *more* than immortal. He has arisen from the ashes of his alter ego, Arnost Rosenbaum – new, invincible, and unrepentant. Hershel has just found him and roused himself into a self-righteous fury about his smug prosperity. It wouldn't be satisfying to challenge an expiring man.

On the other hand, it's entirely possible that Lily Sanderson is exaggerating. Arnold Rose may be suffering nothing more serious than a bad headache. For a headache a person doesn't need to alert the Burial Society. For a headache, Arnold can take a couple of aspirin – something stronger if necessary – and then face his accuser, man to man.

With a simple headache, a person should take responsibility for his sins.

20.

Arnold has a headache, but unfortunately it is not a simple one. It's a crushing pain caused by the extreme elevation of his blood pressure. It is a critical symptom which no analgesic can assuage. While he remains in fierce denial of the gravity of his physical state, his mind is in tumult. It roars and splutters with a confusion of pictures, phrases and long-forgotten melodies. The only coherent thought he can capture through the chaos is that somehow he will come through this. It – whatever it is – will pass, and Arnold will endure.

'I wish that man would hurry and ring back,' frets Helena, who has made several futile attempts to contact the cardiologist.

'It is not an emergency,' Arnold repeats doggedly. 'That bumptious young doctor said *nothing* about an emergency. You're making too much fuss.'

'He said it was urgent – you heard him. He promised we'd hear from Dr Irving very soon.'

'That was only yesterday,' Arnold points out, thinking – can that really be so? It seem he has withstood a hundred years of this passivity, of ingesting Helena's dreadful invalid diet, of being hunted by an old man with a haunting sigh.

'Yesterday was a long time ago – a lot can happen in twenty-four hours,' Helena declares. 'Beryl Klughorn was telling me about a friend of hers who...'

'Don't pester the man,' says Arnold, obstructing her account. If he is subjected to one more case history, he'll lose control.

'I won't. I'll give him one more hour.' She ponders for a moment. 'Oh my goodness – I've just remembered that we're supposed to be meeting here tonight. My museum team. It was organised long before we knew about your condition. I think I'll ask Bernard to ring around and put everyone off – I'm sure he won't mind under the circumstances.'

'There's no need to cancel anything on my account,' Arnold objects. But she is already dialling Bernard's number. In vain. There is no reply.

'How frustrating,' she murmurs. 'Where on earth can he be?'

Bernard is in the synagogue, where he is about to recommence his inspection of the electrical wiring. Hershel has been far from welcoming, hardly bothering to hide his displeasure about the Cantor's arrival. He's still weak from Lily's visit. What has he done to deserve further punishment now? He barely listens to Bernard's florid apologies for his intrusion and his complex explanation for its urgency. Something about an important museum board meeting this evening and the necessity for him to put forward his technological proposals. Which means, of course, that he'll have to complete his on-site review.

'Get on with it,' says Hershel. 'I'll wait for you.' Twenty minutes later he is still tapping his feet impatiently at the synagogue door while the man is meddling inside. 'Excuse me – mister,' he calls.

'One more minute,' answers Bernard, who has climbed up to the women's gallery and seems to be precariously suspended from the railing. Hershel hopes he is qualified for Divine protection for he doubts whether the synagogue insurance policy covers adventure sports. He is about to issue a warning when he sees Bernard awkwardly but safely reaching the ground.

'What potential this place has,' he says, catching his breath and shaking his head. 'I'm sure they're going to leap at my proposals. Apparently, there's a huge amount of interest – Helena *begged* me to make the thing as detailed as I possibly can.'

'Helena?' Hershel asks, feigning ignorance.

'Helena Rose – our Chair. Haven't you met her?'

'Not officially,' says Hershel as though, like royalty, he is constantly subjected to formal introductions.

'You must, you must!' Bernard says rapturously.

'You say the meeting is *tonight*?' Hershel is suddenly alert.

'Indeed it is – it's at her house again. They have the most wonderful property in Onslow Square.'

'I believe so.' He makes his lack of enthusiasm apparent. Then a frown creases his brow. 'She's hosting a meeting with her husband so unwell?'

'Arnold? I saw him just the other day and he seemed perfectly healthy to me.'

'Me too. But I have it on good authority that it isn't the case at all. Lily Sanderson told me.'

'Ah.' Bernard nods slowly. 'She would know.'

'I can't go into detail, I'm afraid,' says Hershel, rather enjoying his role as the bearer of dark tidings and wondering whether this counts as a sin. Not too serious a transgression, evidently, for it galvanises Bernard into a hasty departure.

'I must ring Helena immediately,' he says as he leaves.

'That must be Dr Irving!' Helena jumps up in response to the phone. Ten times during the course of the afternoon she has expressed the same certainty, and on each occasion it has been one of her cronies instead. This time it is Bernard. 'I've been trying to reach you,' she says. 'How lucky you called.'

Arnold tries not to listen for he doesn't think he can tolerate yet another sotto voce reference to her husband's *condition*. He has warned her not to supply anyone with medical details, but the implicit gravity in her non-specific references makes his prognosis sound even worse. He gazes intently at his newspaper, but isolated phrases reach him nevertheless.

'It's such a small world... how strange the way things travel in circles... I'll tell him about it right away.'

When she has concluded the conversation, he tries to pre-empt the predictable goodwill message: 'I know – Bernard sends best wishes.' Arnold is sick to the back teeth of best wishes.

'He does.' She picks up the piece of knitting she has suddenly started. Arnold hasn't seen her knitting since Sandra's last pregnancy, and wonders what role this activity heralds. His nursemaid, perhaps? 'It's really strange,' she muses, 'how quickly news spreads. Do you know how Bernard heard about your condition?'

'How?' Alarm courses through him.

'Hershel told him. Hershel – remember? The synagogue caretaker.'

'I've got that by now,' he says with only a hint of his usual astringency. 'I gather who Hershel is.'

'Well, it was Lily – in her usual unrestrained fashion – who passed it on to Hershel and Bernard happened to pop into the synagogue to measure up or something, and...'

'Helena,' he interrupts, 'this is boring beyond belief.'

She shrugs and counts stitches while he lies back as though beset by deep ennui. But his head has started reeling again and his heart is pounding. Hershel again. Hershel... Hershel. For fifty years he has been out of sight and mind – now suddenly his name is on everyone's lips, in everyone's mind. Isn't there a way, short of murder, to silence him – them – once and for all? Is there any way in which his murder can be organised, justified and concealed? Arnold tries to regulate his breathing. He inhales...exhales... slowly and evenly. But he cannot control his thumping heart. Nor, it seems, can he control Hershel, who has netted him and is relentlessly closing in.

The telephone rings again, and at last it is Dr Irving. 'Finally!' cries Helena. 'We've been waiting for your call. What a relief!'

She pauses for a long while to listen, then solemnly says, 'I see. I'll ask him. One moment, Dr Irving.'

She wants to know whether Arnold is feeling any better. Dr Irving has a particularly crowded schedule this afternoon and would prefer – if at all possible – to see him tomorrow. Having examined Dr Fowles's report, he is concerned but not alarmed about Arnold's condition – but of course the patient is his own best barometer. So, if Arnold is anxious or experiencing a particular sense of urgency…

'I'm not,' he says quickly.

'Are you sure?' Helena covers the mouthpiece and urges him to insist on an immediate appointment, but he pretends not to hear. His fear for his health is immense, yet his desire to remain prone is dominant. He would prefer to die than be forced to his feet.

'I'm positive,' he says, astonished by how convincing he sounds. 'I'm quite confident that the matter can wait till the morning. Another night won't make the slightest difference.' Having managed that speech – brilliantly, under the circumstances – he sinks back again, exhausted. Helena's muted murmuring floats above him and then settles at a point above his ear.

'It's all arranged,' he hears her saying. 'Dr Irving says you're to have a restful evening – I'll see to that – and he'll fit you in tomorrow at ten.'

21.

Arnold is reassured the instant he catches sight of Dr Terence Irving. He is elegantly stooped with silver hair and the whitest hands Arnold has ever seen. *This* is a doctor, he thinks. Young Fowles was conscientious, no denying it. But inexperienced, lacking in gravitas. Dr Irving, on the other hand, commands respect.

'Do come inside, Mr and Mrs Rose,' he says, as though inviting them into his salon. Which his surgery pleasingly resembles, with its fireplaces and fine furniture and oriental rugs. Arnold has always been able to identify a man of discernment and this – his antennae tell him – is one. He feels better already. Observing the air of calm and assurance with which the doctor leafs through his records, he becomes increasingly certain that all the doom-ridden speculation has been in vain. What a fuss for nothing. To think that poor Helena was deceived by that alarmist. Arnold is moved to place an encouraging hand on her knee.

She covers and squeezes it, clearly mistaking the gesture for one of apprehension. 'Chin up,' she whispers.

Irritated, he withdraws his hand, crosses his arms and straightens his back. He remains perfectly still while they wait. Dr Irving, he imagines, has little respect for a man who lacks composure – and, for some reason, it seems important to command his respect.

'Now then...' At last the doctor looks up, beaming genially across the table. 'Let us consider your position.' Which, Arnold learns to his immense relief, turns out not to be as precarious as Dr Irving initially feared. 'Obviously,' he continues in the same unruffled tone, 'one cannot take chances with an organ as crucial as the heart, so I'm recommending a battery of tests. But panic is not necessary. In fact, Mr Rose, it is strictly contra-indicated.'

Arnold slides a sideways glance towards Helena, making sure she has absorbed this. Then he nods firmly. 'I am not the sort of person who is easily alarmed.'

'I can see that,' agrees the doctor approvingly, and draws himself to his feet. 'Now, Mr Rose, if you'd please like to step next door for a couple of tiny procedures?'

Next door, Arnold discovers, is more like a laboratory than a salon. His unease begins to rise again in the stark white surroundings. 'What sort of – er – procedures are you contemplating?' he asks. He struggles to remain outwardly calm while eyeing the technological items ranged round the room.

'Nothing to worry about, nothing at all,' answers Dr Irving, making small dismissive gestures and speaking in a murmur. Arnold's anxiety is soothed away until, almost in a trance, he finds himself stripped to his underwear. Electrodes are attached to various parts of his body. He allows the doctor to guide him across the room, thinking how adaptable he is proving. Yet again. Adaptable and resilient... 'What I'd like to ascertain,' Dr Irving says, 'is how your system responds to physical exertion. This platform here is a treadmill. I shall turn it on very slowly at first. Slowly and gently.'

Arnold places one foot in front of the other with careful precision, aware as he walks that he is remaining in the same place. But keeping up, nevertheless. Easily maintaining the required pace...

'It's all well within your ability,' Sándor Novacek maintained. 'You're a smart young man. Don't quote me, but I imagine you won't be a junior clerk for long.'

How effortless it was. Like breathing. Like taking a leisurely stroll. Left, right, left, right. Adding figures, taking orders – and very soon checking on the addition of others and issuing orders. Charming, promising Arnost Rosenbaum. Young and free. Jewish, admittedly, but an assimilated Jew, an open-minded Jew. One who could discuss without hysteria such matters as usury, Christ-murder, blood libel. An objective Jew, able to evaluate whether or not his people had betrayed Hungary to the godless Russians and would give Slovakia to the Czechs and Transylvania to the Rumanians. A cultured Jew. A different Jew. One who rose like a bubble through the ranks of Novacek's company.

'Excellent,' encourages Dr Irving. 'I'll make it move slightly faster. Do you think you can manage that?'

'With ease,' says Arnold confidently. 'With the greatest ease.'

Upward, upward. A dizzying ascent through the strata of management and out into the executive stratosphere where he stayed in single-minded orbit. Eyes forward, never looking down, for in the darkness far beneath him was a dark-haired mother with her baby boy. A boy who lacked a father. A mother called Rachel with a fatherless child called Miklós.

But progress didn't lie in the murky valleys. He was determined not to avert his gaze. He was afraid that if he looked down he would falter and fall...

'Easy now,' Dr Irving is saying. 'Try and take it calmly, Mr Rose.'

'I'm completely calm.' See? Even under conditions such as these he manages to exude certitude.

'Shall I increase the pace, then?'

'Of course. Go ahead.'

There were vague rumours about things happening to Jews. But everyone assured Arnost that Admiral Horthy would dissuade his friend Hitler from any thought of harming *Hungarian* Jews. Especially Jews like Arnost who shared tables with the rich and influential, eating roast goose and strudel and cream-slices with pastry like butterfly wings.

His stomach was still satisfyingly full on the evening he learnt that Hershel had been conscripted to a forced labour camp. When he read Rachel's letter he felt unaccountably nauseous, and angry with her for unsettling him. 'Miklós and I are now alone,' she wrote. 'When are we going to see you?'

Soon, he answered, swallowing his displeasure. Very soon. He'd come up by train the following weekend. She could count on him. She must count on him.

But the next weekend Madame Novacek threw a last-minute reception in honour of some visiting celebrities. He was needed as a partner for Olga. What could he do? Risk his position, his future – their future? He was sorry…

'Let's try it a wee bit faster,' says Dr Irving. 'Steady, even breaths. You're doing well.'

Things suddenly became tense. The War had begun to lap at their feet and was rising to their ankles. Among the regular guests at Sándor Novacek's villa were growing numbers of German officers and, with the situation so delicate, the presence of a Jew – no matter how cultured or assimilated – became an embarrassment.

'Arnost, I'm afraid you'll have to leave,' Novacek announced one day. 'I've tried everything to prevent this – God knows I've tried.'

'I've resigned from my job,' he wrote to Rachel. 'It wasn't for me, really. I need something more challenging. It might be difficult for a time, financially speaking, but with my excellent connections and references it won't be long before I find something. Being Jewish in Hungary is not a great problem – after all, this is not Austria or Poland.'

He believed it even in March 1944, when the country was invaded by the Germans. He believed it when Adolf Eichmann took up residence in Budapest's Majestic Hotel. He even clung to his conviction a few days later, when Jews were ordered to wear a yellow star. They were prohibited from owning telephones and cars and using public transport. Arnost merely shut his eyes and kept repeating to himself that nothing terrible would happen.

'Excellent,' Dr Irving is saying. 'You're doing even better than I'd hoped. Now I'm going to raise one end of the treadmill. Let us see how you manage on a gentle slope.'

Rumours gathered, buzzing in insistent swarms. Arnost swatted them away, refusing to hear them and declaring himself unafraid. He received a postcard from Rachel. It had been sent from a place called Waldsee. It was a labour camp somewhere in West Hungary. 'We are well,' she wrote. 'We are working. We have everything we need.'

He believed her because he needed to. He was still telling himself that nothing would happen to her – to any of them – for the War would soon be over. The Russians were closing in from the East. The Allies were poised for the right moment to invade Europe and occupy it. The important thing, he told himself, was not to be nervous – to endure with patience – to outlast them.

'Keep it steady, Mr Rose. It seems you're struggling slightly. I think we should stop now. I don't want to push you too hard.'

'I'm fine. Really. I'm managing perfectly.'

'Are you sure? My readings are satisfactory, but you appear out of breath.'

'No. This is easy. It's nothing. I'm feeling fit.'

By autumn 1944, the rumours were darker and uglier. The buzzing had become a cacophony. Not even Arnost could ignore it now. He received a message from Novacek, advising him to disobey Nazi orders to move into a ghetto. Instead, he should approach the Spanish embassy. There, with a few words of Spanish which Novacek was sure Arnost could easily muster, he would find protection.

So it proved. Together with more than a thousand other Jews, he was given false papers and sanctuary in a tall apartment block. The building was protected by the Spanish flag and the warning: 'Do not enter. This building is used by the Spanish State.'

Arnost felt secure. From his hideaway he heard gunfire each night. With rhythmic regularity came pairs of staccato shots and then silence. He tried to disregard the noise. He tried to concentrate instead on the soothing image of the Danube beneath his window. Surely it couldn't be true that Jews were being murdered, their bodies dumped into his beloved river?

Anyway, at least he was safe. And Rachel, too, in her country camp called Waldsee. And Miklós, of course.

The treadmill is raised again. Arnold perseveres. He focuses on the evenness of his breathing and the composure of his countenance. He begins to struggle badly, though. His chest feels too small to contain his hammering heart. His lungs rasp. An ache spreads from his shoulder blades and through his arm.

'Okey-doke,' says Dr Irving.

The belt stops moving. The white room still spins, but at least the ground is now still.

'How do you feel?'

'Perfect.' The ache is receding. It's still there, gnawing at him, but it is certainly not incapacitating. Not for someone like Arnold Rose.

'Any pain anywhere?'

'No. None at all.'

'Excellent. Now, if you'd like to get dressed...'

Helena and the doctor are already deep in conversation when Arnold rejoins them. He feels immoderately glad to have completed his test and emerge from that Siberia of a surgery intact. How good it is to be back in this comfortable and opulent salon.

'I'm not entirely happy,' the doctor is saying.

Arnold wants to tell the man that no one is entirely happy. Ever. It is something he learnt at the age of ten.

'So when would you like him to go into hospital?' asks Helena in a small tentative voice which pierces Arnold's cloak of euphoria and sets his anxiety pulsing again. He has never heard this voice before.

'As soon as I can find a bed – but only for a brief stay. Unless, of course, we decide he would benefit from surgery. By the way, it has become quite routine. You have no idea how many heart by-pass operations are performed up and down the country each day.'

'Is that so?' says Helena in the same unfamiliar tone. 'We don't have to worry about it at this stage, though, do we?'

'Of course not.' Dr Irving directs his calming gaze towards her and immediately adjusts it to include Arnold. 'I particularly don't want *you* to worry,' he tells him. 'Your wife tells me it's your birthday in a couple of days. We won't rush you into hospital before then.' He winks. 'I wouldn't want to spoil anyone's surprise.'

'Surprise?' echoes Arnold sharply.

'It's not *such* a surprise,' simpers Helena, visibly reassured by the doctor's equanimity. 'Just a family celebration.'

And before Arnold can protest by insisting on immediate admission to hospital in spite of – indeed, *because* of – his birthday, Dr Irving pumps his hand and wishes him well and ushers them out of his salon.

'Phew!' says Helena when they are finally at home. She has collapsed onto the sofa, physically drained but emotionally restored. 'I do believe you are safe in that man's hands, Arnold. There was a moment when I began to worry, but on the whole I thought it all went terribly well.'

He doesn't answer. He is limp with fatigue. As if it isn't enough for him to worry about his health and that persistent Hershel – now it appears there's to be a birthday surprise. Didn't Dr Irving say categorically that Arnold shouldn't be worrying at all? Somehow he'll have to summon the strength to voice his objection. A family celebration will push him over the edge. 'Helena...' he begins weakly.

But she's gone. She has recovered her verve and heads for the kitchen – no doubt to re-establish telephonic communication with her friends. Arnold smiles indulgently – then realises he is smiling. Smiling? He ought to be furious. He should be scathing. But something stops him. It is more than debility. It's a disturbing sensation of remoteness from the business of the present. It is as though he's watching the proceedings from a long distance away – peering at his life through a long thin tube and seeing a tiny figure with a telephone attached to her ear... is that Helena, his wife? And who is that small prostrate figure in the armchair?

And those ghostly shapes in the background?

'Helena!' he calls again, distressed.

She doesn't hear him. She is engrossed in her conversation. 'I expected him to be clever, Betty,' she's saying, 'but I was surprised by his humanity, his understanding. Do you know – he specially delayed Arnold's hospital admission so that he could enjoy his birthday at home with us! He says that there is nothing more important than quality of life.'

Quality of life. The phrase floats from her mouth and takes root in Arnold's mind. He repeats it to himself, wondering what it means. In the old days he would have drawn on his mental lexicon for definition and dismissal. Now the words linger like a mantra, meaningless yet imbued with a significance he cannot grasp.

22.

Two days later the phrase is still haunting him. He picks over it compulsively. Is quality material? Is life metaphysical? Never before have matters so abstract seemed relevant to Arnold. When Helena interrupts his reverie with a chirpy 'Happy Birthday!' he is startled into recollection of the dreaded surprise. Which somehow seems less dreadful and certainly less important than the questions crowding his head. He feels the pressure Helena's lips against his cheek and a parcel being pushed into his hands.

'Here's your present,' she is saying. 'I've been awake for ages. I could tell by your breathing that you were awake too.'

He is suddenly conscious of breathing, of the particular way he draws air in and out of his lungs. She knows it, has lived with it and been observing it for forty-two years. She is familiar with its rhythms, its cadences, its distinctive resonance as air whistles back and forth. She knows him intimately, yet doesn't know him at all.

'Aren't you going to open it?'

'Yes – yes, of course.' He begins to fumble with the package, which is securely and elegantly wrapped. It's expensive, he is sure. It is a quality gift.

'Do you like it?' she asks eagerly, almost before he has extracted it from its box. It is a watch. A fob watch made of finest gold. 'It's antique,' she points out. 'It is genuinely old.'

'Like me,' he says, holding it to his ear and listening to its steady ticking. The sound is compelling.

'You'll have to remember to wind it.' She gets out of bed and draws back the curtains. Morning light filters into the room. 'They didn't have microchips when it was made... Isn't it a lovely day, Arnold? I was hoping for your sake that it would be a nice day.' She smiles at him as she bustles round the room. He hears her chattering away – exclaiming, decrying, describing. It occurs to him that the tempo of her conversation is probably as familiar to him as his breathing is to her. Chamber music, he thinks. The modest chords created by long term domesticity. Not the stuff of full-blown symphony but intrinsic to the fabric of day-to-day existence. Can that have something to do with the quality of life?

'Everyone is so much looking forward to this evening,' she says.

'This evening?'

'Oh, Arnold – stop acting so vague. Ever since Dr Irving mentioned it,

I've stopped pretending it's a surprise. It's strictly family, though – I promise. And everyone has sworn to be on best behaviour. I warned Sandra, particularly, to make sure to feed William before they leave home. My theory is that they allow the child's blood sugar to drop too low.'

Sandra. William. Simon, Amy and Evie. Key players in his personal drama. Tiny figures cavorting on a brightly-lit platform with wall-to-wall commentary provided by Helena. And he? Where is Arnold, the co-star, the leading man? Otherwise engaged? In another play, or perhaps in a different act of the same play? One thing for sure is that he cannot be still in Act One, for the curtain has shut. The cast, having taken a bow, has quietly disappeared. Who'd have thought that a feeble old man would have had strength enough to dislodge such a heavy curtain?

'Why don't you lie in for a while? Give yourself a birthday treat,' urges Helena. 'I've so much to do – shopping and cooking. There are also various people I must catch before they go out. You'll be all right, won't you? I'll bring your breakfast upstairs for you – *not* because you're an invalid, Arnold, but because it's a special day. Don't look at me like that! If I can possibly manage to get through all my morning chores, we can have a nice relaxed lunch together and a quiet afternoon.'

She goes bounding downstairs. Arnold listens to her energetic descent and marvels at her unflagging enthusiasm for the minutiae of her life. Then he returns to his musing, accompanied by the measured tick of his new/old watch.

There was a clock in the room he shared with eight people in that apartment block above the river. He never discovered the identity of its original owner. Perhaps it was someone who had lived there previously and abandoned it. So many things were abandoned then. The clock presided over their quarters. Each day, Arnost made sure to wind it so that its tick never ceased. It became his responsibility and his obsession. Helpless in confinement, all he could do was mark time. When gunfire crackled from the Danube, he carefully noted the day and the hour in the diary he kept. It was less of a diary than a numerical record, and confirmed Arnost's strangeness to his companions in concealment. His fixation on numbers, his long moody silences. They had no knowledge of the young man who had charmed his way into the upper reaches of Hungarian society, for he was even deeper in hiding than the Arnost who counted time.

'Has anyone here ever heard of a camp called Waldsee?' he asked one day.

'You had a postcard from there?' someone said in a knowing, measured tone.

Arnost swung to face his respondent, a bearded young man called Leo – a pessimist, a never-ending source of dire predictions and reported atrocities. He was regarding Arnost with an expression even gloomier than usual. 'Who told you I received a postcard?' Arnost asked defensively.

'Plenty of people have had postcards from there,' said Leo, looking away.

'Where is it?' persisted Arnost uncomfortably. And then, when Leo didn't answer, he dared to ask: 'Does it – exist?'

Leo swung round slowly and faced Arnost with a wry half-smile. 'Does fairyland exist?' he asked.

There was no answer to that. Arnost reverted to his diary, where he noted the time.

A few days later Leo wanted to know from whom he'd received the postcard.

'My family,' he answered hesitantly.

'Your parents?'

There was a long pause. 'My – wife,' Arnost managed at last. It sounded so peculiar, coming from his lips. He had not used the term to anyone in Budapest. 'My wife and child.' He choked on the last word.

'Your wife and child,' repeated Leo softly, shaking his head. 'We must pray. All we can do is pray.'

What do they mean by prayer? To whom do they pray – people like Leo and Hershel, who proclaim with such certainty their set of beliefs?

Where has it got them? What happened to Leo after all his devout praying? Soon after liberation he was shot dead by a random Russian bullet. And Hershel? Did any great good fortune come out of *his* piety? Hardly – compared with the blessings that rained on godless, fortunate Arnold. Look at him – without a prayer ever passing his lips, he ends up rich, successful and well married.

And old.

And sick.

And possessed.

'All done,' says Helena, bursting back into the room. 'Arnold, I'm amazed you're still in bed. Lily was asking me about your morale and I had to confess I was a teeny bit concerned. She said that a previously fit person who is suddenly diagnosed as ill should be allowed to go through all the proper stages of grieving. It's loss, you see – the loss of one's health.' She hesitates for a moment, frowning slightly, finding it difficult perhaps to reconcile the lightness of her prattle with the dark presence of her husband in bed. 'Anyway,' she continues bravely, 'I said I thought we'd got beyond anger and denial. Neither of us could remember what came next.'

'Acceptance.' Arnold surprises himself by the alacrity of his response.

Helena is astonished. 'Of course,' she says, pausing to stare at him. 'You're usually scathing about Lily's theories – but even you must agree that she comes up with some perceptive observations from time to time.'

This is going too far. Arnold sits up decisively, swinging his feet to the ground. 'Lily Sanderson,' he says, 'talks crap.'

'Arnold!' Helena laughs nervously. If Arnold's docility is unusual, this descent into vulgarity is bizarre. 'To think that you're the man who locked his daughter Evie in her bedroom for using the word *bloody*... I don't know what's come over you.'

'Nothing. Give me five minutes to dress and I'll be with you downstairs.'

'Good.' She smiles with relief. 'I've prepared the most delicious birthday lunch.'

Normally he relishes each morsel of her poached salmon steak with hollandaise, for which she is justifiably renowned. Today, however, the sight of the flaccid pink flesh with its rich yellow coating is offensive. He manages to load his fork but is unable to lift it towards his mouth. 'I'm sorry,' he says at last to Helena, who is watching him with concern. 'I can't eat.'

'It doesn't matter.' Her expression tightens as she removes his plate and takes it with hers (also largely untouched, he observes) to the kitchen. She returns with the cheese board. 'Arnold,' she says, staring fixedly at a wedge of ripe brie, 'can't we at least *pretend* to be having a nice day?' Her voice has become small and tentative again.

'Why?' he asks with the bemusement of a child to whom adult hypocrisy is suddenly revealed. 'Why pretend?'

She shrugs in confusion, for she has never been questioned about pretence. Weaving its cloth out of little lies has come as naturally to her as breathing. It has seen her through countless committee meetings and more than forty years of marriage. Yet what right has he to challenge her on this issue? He is Arnold alias Arnost, her partner in deception, her master in mendacity. How innocent her white lies seem compared with the darkness of his. She is about to attempt justification, when he rescues her. 'You're right,' he concedes. 'We might as well make the best of things.' He tries to smile.

'That's exactly what I meant,' she agrees happily.

How easily the words slip out. Making the best of things. Keeping a cheerful front. It will never happen.

What if, instead, he had refused to play the make-believe game? What would have happened if, instead of applying verbal Elastoplast to her discomfort, he had said: 'Helena – dear Helena – you go ahead and keep pretending. But as for me, I cannot do it any longer. It has become necessary for me to face the truth. Can I share my truth with you?'

If that had happened, would she now be humming to herself in the kitchen as she gathers the ingredients for tonight's festivities? No, they would still be sitting here over the shards of their shattered illusions. They would be mourning the once-lauded rectitude of Arnold Rose and the lost integrity of their marriage.

'Tea?' she offers, popping her head into the room.

'Yes, please,' he forces himself to say. Cheerfully. 'Then I think I'll take myself upstairs for a brief rest, so that I'll be fresh for this evening.'

'An *excellent* idea,' she says, relief illuminating her face.

23.

Upstairs, dozing, Arnold has a fitful dream of Budapest. The ruins of post-War Budapest, a city bombed, besieged and starved. And he, dazzled by the unaccustomed light, fearful of Russian soldiers, is wandering and seeking and finding nothing. There is nothing left to find. He is desolate. Bereaved. He has lost his beloved city with its promise of prosperity and its lavish hospitality. All he sees are strangers roaming the ravaged streets with hostile faces. All but one. With joy he identifies a single familiar presence. It is Helena. Thank God, *thank God...*

Helena? In Budapest? No – Helena was never in Budapest. He must be – have been – dreaming, hallucinating. Helena is here in London. Arnold is in London. She is touching his forehead and gazing into his face. 'Arnold,' she is saying. 'You were sleeping so soundly – I hate to waken you. It's getting late, though. You had better get up.'

'Late?' he asks, confused. He becomes aware of a ticking sound, an insistent ticking almost into his ear. It is his mellow-gold new/old timepiece reminding him that it is six thirty-four.

'Everyone will be here by seven.' She sounds breathlessly busy and keeps moving round the bedroom. 'The idea is for you to come downstairs after we've assembled.'

'Why?'

'Oh, it's just a surprise that the children have prepared – I'm not meant to let on. How are you feeling, Arnold? You seem slightly more relaxed.' She has bent over him, almost in a position of supplication. He can feel the force of her yearning. She is almost suffocating him with her longing for him to be as he seems.

'I can't,' he whispers.

She draws even closer. 'You can't what?'

What he wants to say is that he cannot do it – be the way he seems – any longer. That he has lost the knack of existing in the present and is floating free. 'I'm very tense,' he says instead.

'Shall I get you a valium?' she offers. 'Dr Irving gave me a few – to tide you over the weekend. He thought you might feel strained, one way or another.'

'No.' His vehemence in refusing sedation takes him by surprise. 'Nothing like that.'

She steps back, equally astonished. 'I was only offering.' She sounds hurt.

'I know,' he says with some remorse, for what other solace does she have at her disposal? All their married life he has sought refuge in numbness and oblivion. He has limited her vocabulary of consolation. He rises to his feet laboriously and sees her watching him, intently studying his every move. Touched by her concern, he reaches out and strokes her cheek – a gesture so uncharacteristically gentle and loving that her hand springs up in amazement to his on her face.

'Oh,' she says. There is silence. She is lost for words – Helena, lost for words? 'You're right,' she manages at last – is that a tremor in her voice? 'We can't have a befuddled birthday boy.'

'Exactly!' He hits a note of confidence that immediately restores her equilibrium. And his own. 'You need to have me bright and alert – the life and soul of the party.'

She laughs, the tension lifted. 'Since when,' she asks ironically, 'has Arnold Rose ever been the life and soul of a party?'

In the bath a few minutes later he ponders on her last remark. Was that regret he detected? Was she implying that he had failed to fulfil her social expectation? He'd always seen himself as – well, not exactly gregarious, but affable. Polished. An asset in company. A man of culture and breeding. But perhaps he was wrong. Perhaps it wasn't purely by choice that they mixed so rarely with other couples. Maybe there was a darker reason why Helena threw herself so strenuously into charity work. Can it be that he's less widely admired than he so long believed? And if so, does it matter?

He hears greetings and high-pitched laughter rising from the floor below. Helena, her children and her grandchildren are creating a self-sufficient noise. Arnold is aware but not resentful of his exclusion. He wonders in an abstract sort of way why he – the focus for this gathering, the *paterfamilias* – feels so distant and extraneous. But he doesn't dwell on it, for it is almost as though he has been dislodged from his perch in the present and is floating, floating…

Back to Nyíregháza. To the train station with its shabby familiarity. So much smaller than he remembered. Tiny. The smell was the same though – the identical acrid odour that once signalled adventure. Now it filled him with nausea and loneliness. Not a single familiar face could he identify – nowhere a flicker of recognition. They were all strangers – even in Yetta's house. Defiant-looking strangers who shrugged and shook their heads when he asked about Rachel.

'Gone.'

'The boy?'

'Gone.'

'Her brother – Hershel?'

No one knew.

This was a nightmare. It wasn't happening, it couldn't be happening. It must be a terrible dream. Yet he was there, knocking on a door, hammering at a door – Yetta's door – hammering until his knuckles bled, but still they refused to open it. Go away, they shouted. Leave us alone. If you don't go away we will call the police.

'Arnold – where are you? We're all waiting for you.'

'I'm on my way down – I won't be long.' He dresses hastily. In the mirror, adjusting his tie, he sees a melancholy old man whom he fails to recognise. Arnost Rosenbaum doesn't look like that and Arnold Rose would never allow himself to appear so ancient and defeated. Who is it then? Who is this sad geriatric?

Downstairs the family has assembled into a semi-circle to greet him. As he appears at the top of the stairs, they launch into a zestfully dissonant rendition of 'Happy Birthday'. Arnold descends slowly, thinking how in the past he'd have been moved to tears by this tableau. He would have paused to extract from his pocket a white linen handkerchief to dab at his eyes. One of the spotless pressed handkerchiefs provided by Helena for use at the opera when the voice of a soprano soared in effortless purity...

But now, although he tries to look pleased, he is conscious of indifference. He is disturbed by this consciousness, for he knows he ought to be stirred by this display of affection. Nevertheless, he is unable to produce an emotional response. 'Thank you,' he keeps saying as they shower him with gifts. 'Thank you – everyone.'

He observes that Evie looks tidy and subdued. She seems to be keeping slightly apart from the others and watches Arnold warily. Helena, however, soon jollies her into conformity ('Come along, darling – no moodiness this evening – it's Dad's birthday!') and chairs the proceedings with her distinctive style.

'In view of the varying ages and degrees of appetite here tonight,' she announces, 'I've decided to serve dinner buffet-style. Please help yourselves to food whenever you are ready – it's all set out on the dining-room table. Once everyone has eaten I shall say a few words. Then we'll light the birthday candles, and finally we'll ask the birthday boy to open his presents. Is that agreed?'

'Unanimously,' says Arnold, mainly because everyone seems to be waiting for him to say something, anything. 'Your mother has many excellent qualities, one of which is an unerring sense of agenda.'

The excessive hilarity that greets his remark is, he recognises, largely relief. He has reassured them of his mental functioning (at least) and can now slip out of the limelight and back to the images in his head.

He was in another railway carriage, this time bound for Nyirbátor. Unintentionally bound, for he'd believed that the train pulling out of Nyíregháza Station was heading back to Budapest. Once the destination was announced, it was too late for Arnost to disembark. So he sat there, speculating on whether fate or an unconscious homing instinct had decreed this return to his birthplace, and wondering what he would find when he got there. He expected nothing but irrationally hoped for everything. In Nyirbátor the sun had once shone and his mother had adored him and Arnost had lavished affection on a warm ball of fluff. On the other hand, in Nyirbátor the sun had set and his mother had preferred someone else above him and cast him out into the cold.

He could hardly bring himself to leave the train when it drew up in Nyirbátor Station. But when he emerged onto the platform and out into the street, it was as though he had come here for the first time. The station was different – the buildings – the streets. Somehow he found himself outside his childhood home – perhaps led here by the same homing instinct. He found an empty ruin.

A stranger walked by. 'Where are they?' asked Arnost, pointing at the deserted house that was once his mother's shop and where sacks of flour had been piled as high as mountain peaks. Where was the yard with its apple trees… the chicken run? The stranger simply stared at Arnost and walked on. He knew further questioning would be futile.

Numbly he caught the next train back to Budapest.

He feels pressure on his arm and opens his eyes to see Evie kneeling at the side of his chair. Her face is serious, purposeful. 'What is it, my dear?' he asks.

She frowns, for he doesn't usually address her thus and she's clearly wary of his sarcasm. She stands up and starts chewing on a nail.

'What is it, Evie?' he repeats in an even gentler tone, and this time she seems reassured. She sighs, shakes her head, then gives a small laugh. It is ironic at first, then – when Arnold joins in out of sheer bemusement – reverts to her old infectious chuckle. He reaches for her hand. 'I have confidence in you,' he says.

She is silent for a moment. 'I was going to tell you…'

'Not now,' he interrupts.

'How ill are you?' she asks abruptly. 'Mother refuses to say.'

'It's difficult…' he admits – realising as he speaks that this is the first time he can remember admitting any inadequacy to his daughter. Until now he has denied fallibility, humanity. How about truth? Perhaps it's time for that too. After all, she is his child – one of his children. 'It's difficult for all of us,' he says after a long pause, for in the end that is the best he is able to do.

It's not enough for her. 'Answer me, Dad – are you very ill?'

'I suspect so,' he says and, having made the acknowledgement, his failing health doesn't seem so bad. It seems irrelevant. There are more important things.

Like the meal, which Helena is determined that he should eat. 'I hate to interrupt, Arnold,' she says. 'Even though you keep telling me you're not hungry, you ought to eat something to keep up your strength. And Evie, there are several vegetarian dishes I prepared especially for you.'

'Helena, *please*,' he begins with a touch of his old irritation. Then he sees her face tensing, her back stiffening and her hands clenching at her sides. It suddenly occurs to him that there is something quite heroic about the way she soldiers on, refusing to see, pretending all is well. There's a kind of bravery in blindness, he decides. Only one kind, though, otherwise the capacity to see would be the sole preserve of the cringing coward. True bravery sees and fears, yet refuses to look away. The all-seeing coward, on the other hand, succumbs to helplessness and despair.

For a time Arnost Rosenbaum, who had seen the night, gave way to cowardice. His shield of blind self-belief had shattered. While he'd been counting minutes in his safe house in Budapest, the world outside had been devastated. Now the clock had stopped, and it seemed there was no safety anywhere. Arnost had become one of the lonely hopeless victims of fate wandering aimlessly through the city, devoid of vanity, ambition, and even fear. All the defences he'd built since the loss of his mother, his chicken, his golden boyhood years, had come crashing down. He roamed from one old haunt to another, weeping with the lack of restraint of one who had nothing left to lose.

Was it sheer luck, then, that brought about his recovery, his rediscovery of the person who knew what he wanted and where he was going? Did random good fortune bring a kind passer-by to administer the first aid that would put poor Arnost Rosenbaum out of his misery and ease into the world the go-getting Arnold Rose?

The passer-by turned out to be bearded Leo, Arnost's melancholy companion in hiding, whose pessimism had been fully justified. He, too, was wandering through the streets of Budapest, but his meandering had a purpose: to collect waifs and strays, casualties into whom he and his fellow workers could inject new life. It was a while before he recognised the slack-jawed, red-eyed figure slumped on a park bench as Arnost. Gently he approached him and, before long, Arnost was following Leo like a stray dog , obediently eating what he was given and sleeping where he was placed.

What quality had enabled Leo to gaze into the abyss without falling? Bravery? True bravery?

'Why are you doing this?' asked Arnost, as he began to recover. Bullets still flew in Budapest. Suspicion and terror still reigned. Yet Leo and his colleagues persevered in their quest for survivors, seemingly unafraid.

'What else can we do?' Leo would respond.

'But *why*?' persisted Arnost. He was growing stronger each day, and with his strength came the restoration of his ego. As his confidence increased, his questions diminished. He was saved. He was entitled to be saved. He recalled with revulsion the pathetic creature he'd once allowed himself to become, and this revulsion spread to those he blamed for his state and even to those who had witnessed it. Including Leo.

When Leo, one day, was killed by a random bullet, Arnost – who cried out when he heard, as though the bullet had pierced him too – quickly collected himself. He set his face, squared his shoulders, and told himself that he was now quite free. Unimpeded by the obligations of kindness, of love. Now that everyone was gone, he would make a fresh start. He was young and strong and would stride ahead.

He would only look ahead.

Helena is turning from him and walking away. 'Don't go,' he calls in panic.

She swings round, alarmed. 'What is it?'

'Helena...'

'Arnold, what is it? What's the matter?'

He cannot tell her. He doesn't really know. 'Sit here for a moment – please – by my side.'

It was easy once he had planned his route. But then Arnost had always been a clever navigator, a one-way traveller par excellence. How smoothly he had moved from Nyirbátor to Nyírgháza and onto Budapest, shedding dross along the way lest his progress be impeded. And now, after a minor disruption, he was on the road once more. He had settled on a destination remote enough to offer him a new beginning.

'Why England?' the various officials he approached wanted to know.

'Why not?' he answered. He had always admired things English and had learnt the language as part of his self-improvement programme. He loved the crispness of its words, its pliant subtlety. Arnost had fixed upon England and would go to any lengths to acquire a visa and a job. He produced the glowing letter of recommendation from Sándor Novacek, which he had carefully preserved through the War. Was that enough?

The official hesitated. Many people boasted good references. They didn't mean much.

Arnost steeled himself, willing away the knot that tightened in his stomach. How about the fact that he was a Jewish victim of war, a bereaved husband, a bereaved father? Would *that* count?

Ah, they said. In *that* case...

'Helena, would you please open a window? I need fresh air.'

'Of course.' She takes his hand. Hers feels steady and cool. 'Simon,' she calls.

Simon? Who is Simon? Who are all these people? Why are they making such a noise when all he wants is stillness... peace?

They told him he was lucky. A fortunate young man indeed. He agreed with them, although he didn't believe in luck. He couldn't afford to. Chance, they said, had brought them a letter from an English benefactor, a Jewish industrialist call Ivan Rothman, who was particularly seeking to give sanctuary and employment to a survivor with experience in the textile industry.

'Why did he do it?'

'What, Arnold? I thought you wanted the window open, so I asked Simon.'

'Ivan.'

'*Ivan*?'

'Ivan Rothman.'

'You mean *Daddy*? What on earth makes you think about Daddy now?'

'What made him suddenly offer his patronage to someone out of the blue like that? A stranger like me?'

'You remember what Daddy was like?'

'No. Hardly.'

'That's true – you didn't get the chance to know him properly. He died so soon after you arrived. He was a... It was kindness, Arnold. Simply kindness.'

Kindness? A new word? Surely not. It is ancient, as old as time. Yet it isn't one that he has examined much, for it is not the most glamorous word. But now that it has been presented to him, he rubs away the dust and something infinitely precious is revealed. 'Kindness,' he murmurs, and Ivan Rothman's face appears before him. And Leo's. And Sándor Novacek's. And that of Hershel Fine.

She squeezes his hand.

There was the girl, Rothman's daughter, who invited him into their home and into her life with the offer of food and stability. Was that kindness? He accepted, for he saw her steadiness and stoicism, the unflinching way she took care of her father during his last dying days. He felt safe with her. She would never let him down; he would never give her reason to let him down. He would bury his ghosts and start afresh. Farewell to Arnost Rosenbaum and greetings to Arnold Rose – a respected and successful man.

But *kind*? Has he been kind?

'Helena, I...' he begins – and stops, for he sees fear in her face, and he too becomes frightened, aware of his vulnerability. He needs to be rescued again. He needs to be loved. 'Help me,' he whispers.

She keeps a tight grip on his hand and applies her other palm to his forehead. He shuts his eyes, aware of her determination for him to be well and his own desperate longing to be saved. But he knows that whatever compassion she musters will not be enough to stop the raging in his head, his chest, his dreadful aloneness. This time there is to be no deliverance. 'Arnold,' she is urging, 'shall I get the doctor? Children, stay calm – there's no need for panic. Perhaps someone should try and reach Dr Irving, though. You'll find his emergency number...'

He stops her. He silences her with a finger pressed to her lips. A steady purposeful finger – for he has suddenly grown calm. He is floating, drifting in a bubble. There is pain in this bubble, he is awash with pain. The sound of rushing water is all about him – yet there is a centre, an eye in the storm that seems luminously clear. How blissful it will be when he sheds the pain and seals himself in that haven. When he becomes the haven – home at last.

He can't though. Not yet. They are making too much noise.

'Everyone keep calm. He'll be fine. Simon, did you get hold of Dr Irving?'

That voice... he knows it from somewhere... but cannot place it.

'Arnold, look at me – talk to me. Does it hurt anywhere? Tell me – please?'

He knows her but doesn't. Perhaps he once dreamt about her, which accounts for that disturbing familiarity. No, it isn't that. There is something… something more… the other faces gathered round him… he's sure he recognises them from somewhere. Why don't they take away the pain and stop the noise? He needs peace.

'Arnold,' she is saying in that same shaky-calm voice, 'we've sent for an ambulance. Dr Irving says you must try and keep as still as possible.'

The words strike him like hailstones, the wind roars, a child sobs.

A child? Sobbing?

'Sandra, please will you take William and Rebecca out of the room. This is neither the time nor the place for them to be quarrelling. Rebecca, give William his car back at once!'

The child sobs harder. It is unbearable. He cannot lie here, helplessly hearing it pouring out its sorrow, loneliness and futile anger. Stop, he says – or thinks he says. Please stop. He seeks the source of that agony in the alien cluster around him, and his eyes rest on a small boy. A boy abandoned, his wailing flooding the room. With all his strength, the last of his strength, Arnold pushes aside the hand holding his and tries to get to his feet. The pain is searing but he has to do this, he cannot let the child cry any longer.

'Miklós,' he whispers, lunging towards him.

Then he falls.

24.

Hershel, meanwhile, is deep in thought. He's been immersed in it for days, has hardly closed his eyes. When he has, he hasn't slept. The same eternal questions are plaguing him, but now he has an inkling that – please God – he is on the brink of finding answers. Each time an answer hovers into sight, however, the question eludes him. Certainty about anything remains tantalisingly and frustratingly out of reach.

The Lord, he thinks, must be laughing at his mental contortions. He hopes the laughter isn't mocking and that his Maker values Hershel's tenacity. At least. It must count for something, the way he perseveres with his life's task and makes the most – in his cerebral way – of his allotted span. On the other hand, maybe in God's eyes thinking isn't living. Thinking is thinking – living is doing. Being. It's an active condition, while Hershel has been passive. More lived against than living. Certainly more sinned against.

The rabbis spoke about the deeds of the fathers being a sign to the children. Neither the thoughts nor the ideas – just the deeds. Which disqualifies Hershel on both counts, being neither a doer nor a father. Life, he decides, has taught him impotence. Like a person caught in a long and violent storm, he took refuge in the only shelter that seemed safe – his thoughts. And now, long after the storm has moved on to devastate other landscapes, Hershel remains in hiding.

Unlike Arnost/Arnold, who – for better or for worse – managed to keep doing, doing, doing. He sinned maybe and fathered certainly. But Arnost/Arnold didn't settle for the thinker's corner. *He* certainly isn't afflicted with inertia.

And where has this got him? Who prevails in the end – the doer or the thinker? Who knows? Hershel comes to three conclusions: the first is that every train of thought he ever takes seems to end with Arnost; the second that, unless he resolves this interminable rumination, he'll go mad. Certifiably mad. Instead of the Menorah Home, he'll wake up one morning in a psychiatric ward. Finally, he decides that the only way to end this fixation is to face his antagonist, for better or worse. He has already tried to bring this about in his typically quiescent way, but cannot wait any longer.

The time has come… finally… with heavy dragging feet… for Hershel Fine to make a move. He has the address, thanks to Lily Sanderson, so if he wants to save his sanity he can't afford to delay a moment longer.

Being Hershel, he procrastinates; a single resolution isn't enough to reverse a lifetime of passivity. He plans and re-plans his route, eats a fortifying breakfast, and then sits down for a while before setting off – all perfectly justifiable measures. How can a person embark on an expedition without a map in the pocket and a meal in his stomach? As for the sitting down: it's a gesture said to deflect the Evil Eye from a journey. Not that Hershel is superstitious but – who knows? Why take chances?

At last, when he cannot find a single reason further to postpone his departure, he steps into the street. He suddenly realises how frightened he is. His mouth is dry from fear. Cars speed by, buses rumble, people push past him with purposeful strides. Hershel, breathing in short gasps, has to fight an urge to retreat to his flat. He feels like a fish out of water.

Like the fish in the rabbinical story who is swimming in a great rush along a stream when he is spotted by a scheming fox. 'What's the hurry, Mr Fish?' calls the fox. 'Who's chasing you?' 'A fisherman with a net,' gasps the fish. Suggests the fox: 'Why not come up here on dry land for safety?' He thinks he's so clever, his mouth's already watering. But the fish isn't going to be fooled so easily. 'What are you talking about, Mr Fox?' he says. 'If I'm frightened in *my* element, think how much more afraid I'll be if leave it!'

Hershel thinks that maybe he too should have remained in his element. Is madness such a terrible thing? What is he looking for – *real* trouble? He spots a wooden bench. A nice solid and currently unoccupied bench dedicated to the memory of... he can't make out the faded inscription, but decides to sit down as a gesture of commemoration. As it happens, he also doesn't mind taking the weight off his feet for a couple of minutes. In addition, he needs to pause and consider.

And reconsider.

How many days, weeks and months did he sit like this at the side of the road on his way back to Nyíregháza? Paralysed. Wanting time to cease. Afraid to have his worst fears confirmed. At last he dragged his battered body into the town and along the streets and, dizzy with dread and fatigue, hammered on the front door of his house.

'Gone,' they said.

'Everyone?'

'Everyone.'

It was far worse than his most pessimistic speculations. Now all he wanted was to die. 'Take me,' he begged God. 'Please be kind and take me now?'

What a request. Since when had God been kind? Would a kind God have brought about such a situation in the first place? Was there any kindness in a God who had engineered or even allowed the suffering of His people, the best of His people. Rachel... Miklós... thousands, millions more. Hershel had heard talk of Auschwitz but didn't want to believe such a thing. It was true, though. They had thought, poor innocents, that they were bound for the country, for the salubrious air of Waldsee. And instead...

'Tell me, Lord,' Hershel pleaded – deranged with grief, 'how is it possible for me to believe in Auschwitz and in You?'

It took a while for him to reach the conclusion that it is not an either/or situation. Auschwitz was Auschwitz and God is God. Anyway, is there anything else in which Hershel can believe? It's like water – if a person drinks once from a polluted stream does he desist from drinking altogether and die of thirst?

Hershel didn't die. He had survived on starvation rations and hard labour. He'd outlived several life sentences and a death march. Now, through the intolerable after-time and despite his persistent entreaties to God to let him die, he remained quite alone and full of despair – but alive.

And although people say that life means hope, the aphorism has never applied to Hershel. He lost hope then and never recovered it. Belief is different. To Hershel, God exists in the pumping of his heart, the working of his lungs, and the comprehension of his mind. He is life itself. And while hope would be a welcome bonus, it's a luxury he's learnt to manage without.

'Nice warm day.'

Hershel jumps. The space alongside him on the bench has been filled by an elderly woman in a heavy grey coat. 'So-so,' he mutters, his tone signalling his reluctance to talk.

But his companion persists: 'Did you see the forecast, though? Cold and cloudy with scattered showers. That's what they said.'

'And so?' He shrugs. Doesn't he have more important things on his mind than the weather? Why won't this woman let him be?

'And so,' she echoes, 'here I am in my winter coat almost expiring from the heat.'

'Take it off then,' he suggests as courteously as he can.

'Then I'll have to lug it round all day. Feel the *weight* of it.'

'Oh, I don't know,' he says wearily. Such a problem she thinks she has. *Such* a problem.

'I keep telling myself not to take any notice of weather forecasts,' she grumbles. 'But what else is there?' She grows silent, pensive, a sweltering mound of grey wool, betrayed by her faith in meteorology. 'There's always my horoscope, I suppose,' she continues, almost to herself. 'I used to be quite lucky with that. There was a patch when that Madame whatever-her-name-was in *The Sun* managed to get it spot-on for weeks. Then she went off. They all do, eventually. But weather forecasting's a science, isn't it? It should be more reliable than gazing at the stars.'

'It should,' Hershel agrees, struck by the wistfulness in her voice. It occurs to him how much yearning there is in the world – the outer world that stretches infinitely beyond the boundaries of his experience, as well as countless inner worlds. So many fears, so many tragedies. What longings, for instance, lie in the heart of this poor perspiring woman? What answers is *she* seeking? 'Reliability is all very well,' he says, looking at her properly for the first time and seeing a life, a whole life. 'But if everything were predictable…'

'Wouldn't that be wonderful?' she interrupts, clearly pleased to have captured his attention.

'You think so? I'm not sure.'

'But why? I'd have been suitably dressed for the weather. I like to *know* what's in store.'

'I myself,' says Hershel, 'prefer to keep the possibilities open. One never knows.'

'That's the thing,' she breaks in excitedly – but Hershel silences her.

'Forget the weather,' he says, unable to hide his impatience. 'I'm talking about the dream. The possibility of something better – if not in this life then in the next. A person has to have a dream.'

She stares at him peculiarly. Has he stepped beyond the bounds of this particular conversation?

'I'll be on my way then,' she says, gathering her parcels and buttoning her coat.

He watches her leaving with a sense of regret. Surely he isn't sorry about the departure of a rather irritating stranger? No, it's something more, something that takes him way, way back to a conversation with a young boy tormented by betrayal and loss. Perhaps he might have learnt something from that boy, from this woman, if he hadn't repelled them through his arrogance. Anyway, how could he have spoken with such certainty about the importance of dreams when *all* he has ever managed was to dream?

Anyway, now he is at last risking reality, finally stepping away from his endless introspection. In search of what? The ghost of Arnost Rosenbaum, who discovered at an early age that dreams achieve nothing, or the sick shell of the stranger they call Arnold Rose? What will he find when he reaches the house in Onslow Square?

He finds Lily Sanderson. More accurately, he almost crashes into her. She is retreating from the front door with a hefty casserole dish in her arms when Hershel approaches. And before he knows it, he finds himself holding the dish, staggering under its weight, and hearing that Arnold, poor Arnold...

'What happened?'

'He collapsed. Last night. His heart. I heard about it this morning, so I rushed over with this.'

'Is he...?' Hershel has to put the dish down for his heart is thudding.

'He's hovering, apparently.' Lily gazes at him with solicitude. 'Oh dear, this must be awful for you. And you've come all this way. You must have had a premonition. I believe people have a sense when someone close to them...'

'Hovering?' he asks nervously.

'Well, I didn't speak to Helena herself – she hasn't moved from his side, poor thing. But Betty heard from one of the children that at first they thought he was... finished. Then he rallied in the ambulance and I believe that since then it's been touch and go. I'm not exactly sure what the position is now. I'll try and get to the hospital this evening.'

'Which hospital?' Hershel hears himself asking, despite his fervent wish to retreat from this drama. He wants to go back to his flat. What business does Hershel Fine have with hovering Arnold Rose and his pushy wife?

Lily identifies the hospital, sparing no detail. She knows hospitals like the back of her hand. She assures Hershel that Arnold, thank heaven, is in the best institution that money can buy. 'As it happens,' she adds, 'I'm driving past it on the way to my osteopath, so I can drop you off – I tried to cancel the appointment but Marcus insisted I keep it. It might seem selfish, but for once...'

'Not at all,' he murmurs, stepping alongside her with the casserole dish balanced in his arms again. Like a sleepwalker. Left, right, left, towards her car. As he reaches it, he recoils. 'Actually...' he begins.

But she opens the door and urges him inside. 'It's no trouble, Hershel – none at all. As I said, it's on my way. I'm delighted to help you.'

She starts the engine, reverses into the street and joins the stream of traffic. He sits back limply, powerless to resist.

That was how it was after he witnessed the wreckage of his life in Nyíregháza. He became a human form without a will, a rag-doll. Again he was at the roadside, a piece of flotsam at the mercy of chance. Random vehicles plucked him up then dropped him – a few wagons, a lorry, an army truck, all heading in the direction of Budapest. They carried him closer and closer to the capital, where he remained alive through the same fortuity that had led him there. Bullets rained down in the streets; the Russians gathered prisoners for shipment to Siberia. Criminals proliferated in the chaos. But nothing touched Hershel. He tried to summon his own demise. Deliberately he placed himself in positions of danger, crying out to be snatched from existence. But God wasn't ready for him. Not yet.

One day Hershel found himself in a place with beds and food and kind faces. There was one, in particular. A young bearded man called Leo, whose compassion found a path through Hershel's apathy. But he suddenly disappeared – it happened all the time – and the apathy returned. An impenetrable buffer settled over his mind, his emotions and his unwieldy body. His senses were dulled. He was beyond despair. When someone mentioned that a charitable organisation in England was offering refuge to an orthodox Jew, he nodded blankly. They took his gesture as acceptance, explaining that he would have to take the position of synagogue caretaker in exchange for safety and peace. He didn't mind, one way or another. Asylum in a house of God was probably as good as it would get.

'Here we are!' Lily says, bringing her car to a screeching halt.

A terrible driver, thinks Hershel, who has spent the short journey clutching the dashboard. After so long wishing his life would end, he is remarkably keen to reach this destination in one piece.

'Give them all my fondest love,' she trills, as he leaves the car as quickly as he can. 'Tell Helena I'll try and catch up with her later.'

25.

As he enters the hospital he is aware of being empty-handed. Undefended. Even Lily's casserole would have been something to grip. Not that she didn't try to foist it upon him, but even in his weakened state he managed to resist. Which is just as well, for he sees that people are holding flowers and fruit and plastic bags. An old man bearing an earthenware dish would look odd indeed. He *is* odd, though. A misfit. Forever a stranger in a strange land.

Hershel shifts uncomfortably from foot to foot. Why has he come here? Why didn't he resist when Lily escorted him into her car? Why doesn't he leave now? Why doesn't he turn around and head back home? *Home*? That's a good one.

'Can I help you, sir? You seem lost.' A young woman with a scrubbed face and a badge on her chest that says 'Visitor Adviser' has placed herself squarely in front of him. She has Lily's look of zealous solicitude and Hershel wonders if there is a sudden proliferation of the breed. Or maybe there is something about him that attracts them. *Is* he lost? If so, she has found him and is determined not to let go. 'I know exactly how you feel,' she is saying. 'Visiting someone in hospital can be extremely stressful. But it's much better to talk about it than to keep it inside.'

'Is that so?' says Hershel. In his experience talking leads to nothing but a sore throat and who needs that in a hospital? In two minutes they'll have him in a bed, next thing a knife, next thing... 'Actually, I'm in a rush today. Another time maybe?'

She nods with eager sympathy, and Hershel pictures himself as her prey pinned helplessly beneath her compassion. Someone else – someone like Arnold Rose for instance – would be marching to the counter and articulating his business loudly and clearly. Someone like *Arnold Rose...*

Hershel winces at the recollection of the reason for his presence. Arnold Rose is not in a position to demand anything from anyone. Not now. And while Arnold – Arnost, go-getting Arnost – is lying helpless somewhere in this building, Hershel remains on his feet, in full command of his faculties. A victim no longer. Not today.

'Excuse me,' he says with an assurance that takes him by surprise. It evidently flusters the Visitor Adviser as well, for as he walks past her to the reception desk, her nose reddens and her mouth opens and shuts soundlessly.

'Rose?' The woman behind the counter peers at a computer screen.

Hershel concentrates on maintaining his air of assurance and standing as tall as he can. It's a strain. 'Mr Arnold Rose,' he repeats, in the most authoritative voice he can muster. His back is beginning to ache quite severely.

At last she locates him. 'Ah,' she said. 'Here he is. Or at least as far as I know he's here. The problem is that he's listed as an Intensive Care patient and visitors are strictly limited. Do you actually want to see him?'

He cannot think of anything he wants less. His resolve weakens, his spine begins to slump, but he catches himself. 'I do,' he says firmly. 'I'd like to see Mr Rose.'

'And you are?'

'Hershel Fine.'

'And you are?'

'I told you already. Hershel F...'

'Your relationship, please.'

'My *relationship*?' he demands, offended. 'As it happens, miss – not that it's exactly your business – I'm a bachelor.'

For the first time since the start of their exchange she takes her eyes off the screen. She rolls them and scrutinises Hershel. 'Your kinship with the patient is what I'm after,' she says coldly. 'Only close relatives are allowed to see Mr Rose.'

'I see.' He lapses into thought.

'So *are* you?'

'Am I what?'

'Are you or are you not closely related to Arnold Rose?'

He ponders for a while. Isn't it strange how over all the years and during all his rumination he has never before considered his own ties with Arnost? He has perceived him as Rachel's husband, Miklós's father, and now husband to the elegant Helena. But what was he – what is he still – to Hershel? 'As a matter of fact,' he says, shaking his head in disbelief, so novel is this idea. 'As a matter of fact he's my brother-in-law.'

'Ah, well then...'

Carefully, accurately, he follows her instructions to the eighth floor ICU. He presents himself to the Sister-in-Charge as a fully accredited close family member, Mr Rose's brother-in-law, no less. But she's not impressed.

'Mrs Rose hasn't mentioned a brother-in-law,' she tells him.

'Would I lie about such a matter?' he asks, now exhausted, beyond trying to be impressive, beyond trying to be anything at all. 'Do you think that a person would come to a place like this for pleasure? Maybe I wouldn't have chosen Mr Rose for my brother-in-law, but I can assure you that's who he is.'

She studies him with narrowed eyes. 'You can see him for five minutes only,' she says at last. 'It's along the corridor, the fourth door on the left. If Mr Rose is asleep, he is not to be disturbed.'

'How is he?' Hershel asks. Is this happening? Is he finally about to enter Arnost's presence – with a warning that he must not be (God forbid!) disturbed? To the bitter end, in sickness and in health, Arnost Rosenbaum shouldn't be disturbed? Hershel has stopped expecting justice, but this is…

'He's a very sick man. Critically ill. He had a very bad night but seems much calmer now. His wife has been with him all the time.'

'I see,' says Hershel, wondering if this dutiful Helena knows she is the second wife. Hershel has seen her only once and immediately identified her as a bossy socialite – exactly the sort who would fall for his suave charm. Different in every way to his sister Rachel – yet she too would have remained at his side till the end. 'He's lucky,' he says softly, marvelling at how Arnost has inspired such devotion – at least twice.

He pauses at the doorway to locate the bed. The ward is brightly lit – inappropriately so, for the sick. But perhaps when one has reached the outer edge of sickness the glare doesn't matter. It makes it easy for Hershel to discern attentive Helena, leaning over her husband. She doesn't stir when Hershel advances. She is engrossed in the patient, her head close to his, listening to his every breath.

Her husband. Arnold. Arnost. Is he the prostrate form tube-tethered to that high bed? Is the thin pulsating line on the screen all that remains of his life force? Is this what is left of the boy who seduced his sister, then betrayed and deserted her? Is this the father who abandoned his son, the flamboyant man who prospered in England? Can a person be reduced to – this?

And the wife? What is crossing her mind as she stoops over him, stroking his limp hand? Memories, perhaps, of the man he was – or at least the man she saw? Did her vision include his treachery, his dark side? Would she be sitting here so attentively if she knew?

A spasm of purest rage runs through Hershel. He wants to take this good wife Helena by the shoulders and drag her away – to blast into her face the truth about the man she married. How unfair it is that after all, after everything, Arnost should be lying here, dying here, going out as someone's beloved, when Rachel and Miklós... the brutality, the fear, the pain they must have suffered.

But what purpose will be served by a furious exposition now? Look at him: his face is blank and his body quite still. The sister said he'd had a bad night. Was he frightened maybe? Tortured by guilt – regret – dread? In the end, loving wife or not, Arnost will be alone. Soon it will be between him and his Maker. The world of the living and the once-lived will be irrelevant. Neither money nor charm will buy him a smart enough lawyer for the heavenly trial.

Hershel is suddenly exhausted by his emotions. He sighs. A long sigh that seems to melt into the hiss of the machinery and fade away behind the electronic pips marking the beat of Arnost's heart. She doesn't seem to notice the sigh and is still unaware of his presence. But Arnost's face twitches. Hershel is sure of it. Is it a flicker of recognition?

She sees it too. So intently is she watching him that she observes even this fleeting sign of animation. She bends her face even closer to his and murmurs something. A word. A name. A name?

Hershel leans forward in puzzlement, in disbelief. He holds his breath to hear better, to make sure he isn't making a mistake.

'Arnost,' she is whispering, 'darling Arnost – don't die.'

Quietly, very quietly – now he doesn't want her to see him for he feels like an intruder – he leaves the room, the buzzing glare. The nightmare. 'Arnost...' she said. The sound of her uttering his name, his real name, echoes in his head. The softness of it, the love of it. She loves him. She really loves him.

How can she, though? She doesn't know his capacity for betrayal.

Yet she called him by his Hungarian name, the badge of identity he cast off when he became Arnold Rose.

But that's probably just a term of endearment. She can't know.

He waits, although there seems little point in lingering. Not now. He keeps telling himself he should leave. He has no place here, he should find a bus or taxi – or even, if all else fails, surrender to a Visitor Adviser. But he cannot move. Like a statue, he sits on a chair in the corridor and waits.

The sister passes a few times, glancing at him enquiringly at first, then ignoring his presence. It's as though he has become one with the white walls, the steady bleeping, the background hum and the voice whispering 'Arnost' repeating in his head.

At last she appears. When he sees her – a weary figure leaning against the wall and cradling her forehead – he knows why he waited. He has to talk to her. He has to know.

He stands up, coughing discreetly, but she doesn't respond. 'Excuse me,' he says.

She turns to him, puzzled, slightly annoyed.

'Mrs Rose?'

'Do I...?' she begins.

'My name is Hershel Fine.'

She frowns. 'I don't think we've met.'

'Mrs Rose, I came to see your husband. I knew him – long ago.'

She considers for a moment. 'Oh – I remember. I think I remember. Aren't you the caretaker, the person Lily...?'

'That's right. You know all about me then? Your husband explained?'

'My husband...' Her voice tails off. She seems bewildered, shaken to the core, not at all the smug society lady Hershel anticipated with such scorn. He is sorry for her suddenly – truly sorry. After all, *she* hasn't done anyone any particular harm.

'His illness – did it happen suddenly?' he asks gently.

She shrugs. 'I don't think he's been well for some time. It's hard to know, though, with Arnold. He's not very – forthcoming.'

'He told you about me, though? About who I was... am?'

She shakes her head. 'No. He's never spoken about his past – except in general terms, of course.'

'You called him "Arnost".'

She looks at him sharply. 'How do you know?'

'I heard. I was inside there for a little while, watching you – and him. With permission, of course. I didn't want to disturb you.'

'You saw him? He looks awful, doesn't he? I'd better get back there – the doctor's examining him. I'm so afraid of what he'll say.'

'Is that what you usually call him? Arnost?'

'No,' she says. 'Never. Not aloud. I don't think he's even aware that I know it. As I said, we never talk about the past. I must go back to him now, though, Mr...'

'Hershel.'

'Sorry – my head's in such a muddle. It's been a terrible time.' She presses her temples, struggling with her fatigue and distress. 'Perhaps I should sit down for a minute. I'm sure they'll call me if necessary.'

He helps her to a chair. They sit in silence for a while.

'How did you learn it, then?' ventures Hershel. 'The name.'

'I've always known it. Almost as long as I've known him.'

There is another long silence before he asks: 'Is there anything else you know?'

She doesn't answer for several seconds. Then she tells him in a low, steady voice that she knows her husband was married before, that he had a wife and child who died at Auschwitz. It was something that she and Arnold never discussed, for it was understandably too painful for him to talk about.

'How did you learn about it then?' Hershel asks. 'How did you find out?'

Her father, she explains, brought Arnold here from Hungary after the War. He didn't live to see his daughter married but when, shortly after his death, Helena sorted his papers she found a letter of appeal from an Hungarian refugee agency. It included details about several tragic cases – among them Arnost Rosenbaum, who was widowed and rendered childless by the Nazis.

'I see,' says Hershel. 'And you asked Arnost – Arnold about it?'

'I tried at first. But it upset him. It seemed to upset him so badly that I thought it was better to keep silent.'

'You've been married to him all these years and you didn't speak?'

'Forty-two years,' she says, straightening her back and regaining some of her authority. 'We did speak. We spoke about everything but that.'

He is perplexed. This taboo is something he cannot understand. 'But surely you were curious – at least?'

'At night,' she says, 'I watched his restlessness – I heard him talking in a strange language, moaning. I knew that there was another life, a whole world, that was his. Only his. If he had chosen to share it with me I'd have listened. Instead he chose silence and I – I felt bound to honour his silence. There are some things that are better left unsaid.'

'You must care for him greatly,' Hershel observes, unable to repress the ignoble thought that the man doesn't deserve such unqualified love. But perhaps with love – as with most things in Hershel's experience – entitlement doesn't count.

'I do.' She agrees as decisively as she probably uttered her marriage vows all those decades before. For better or worse.

A woman of valour, thinks Hershel, with grudging admiration. He takes her hand and holds it for a moment, then slowly rises to his feet.

Outside, he steps into the roar of traffic, the bustle of commuters, newspaper vendors calling and beggars entreating. Even above the noise, Helena's soft-spoken affirmation resonates in his head.

'I do.'

As he reaches the corner, Hershel turns to look back at the hospital building, a drab mass almost merging into the leaden sky. He glances upward, offering a wry smile to the Maker who has led him through so many tortuous texts in his quest to understand belief. Now he knows that it can rest in the gentle silence held by a wife, year after year. As simple as that, and as infinitely complicated.

Heavy raindrops start falling, but Hershel doesn't move. He watches as the hospital windows come aglow in the darkening afternoon.